# TEMPTED BY HER RESCUER

## BROTHERHOOD PROTECTORS WORLD

## CHRISTINE GLOVER

Twisted Page Press LLC

# BROTHERHOOD PROTECTORS
## ORIGINAL SERIES BY ELLE JAMES

### *Brotherhood Protectors Series*

*To all the people who dream big and reach for the stars!*

# CHAPTER 1

REAGAN HARLOW THOUGHT Virginia winters were cold but when she stepped out of her rental SUV in Eagle Point Ranch's parking lot at noon, the blast of frigid air went straight through her coat and literally froze her to the bone. "Remind me again," she said to her assistant who joined her. "Whose idea was it to do a holiday cooking show in Montana?" She hugged herself to preserve whatever heat remained in her body.

"You," he replied.

"Right." She'd agreed to do the show after her producer set up the premise. How could she say no when landing this coveted At Home Network's gig after winning a grueling competition only a year ago? "*Cooking Thyme's* reunion with the runner-up at this ranch is supposed to bring homespun holiday cheer to the viewers."

Much to her over-protective brother's chagrin. He'd always looked out for her, stopping bullies and later, grilling potential boyfriends. But ever since her husband had died, he'd hovered over her worse than a helicopter parent.

"A lot of our viewers thought you and Owen were an item off screen."

"The guy's smart, charming and irresistible to legions of women, but he's a bit too old for me."

"He's only forty-five."

"Like I said, I prefer men closer to my age and I haven't even hit thirty yet." Sure, Owen had intrigued her with his ready wit and boundless energy. His creativity in the kitchen had wowed her too. "But it'll be good to see him again. He taught me a lot during the competition." His family's five-star restaurant in New York City had garnered celebrity guests with his innovative, signature dishes.

"Yeah. For a while there, we thought the viewers would vote for him to win," Eric said as they made their way up the stairs. "But you won them over with your genuine, down home attitude."

"I'd like to think my cooking had something to do with it too," she said wryly.

"Your recipes were easier to incorporate into everyday life. And they were delicious."

Her cell phone buzzed in her purse. She withdrew it and read the screen. Mentally, she rolled her eyes and sent her brother's call into voicemail. No way would she give him another chance to talk her out of doing the live show.

"Ugh," she said, jamming her iPhone back inside the crossbody bag. "I swear he's worse than my parents."

Eric held open one of the ranch resort's knotty pine doors. "He's just trying to make sure you're safe."

She swept past the wreath hanging from a bright Christmas tartan ribbon. "Colton doesn't even live in the United States," she said as she strolled inside. Not since he'd taken an assignment overseas in Italy. Not that she begrudged him the new life he'd carved out for himself with his wife. "And I'm a grown ass woman who doesn't need him mother-henning me."

Everyone deserved happiness. But she'd be damned if she let her big brother meddling mess with her goals and ambitions. She'd already lost the life she wanted with her high school sweetheart. Now, still alone after her husband's sudden death before she even turned twenty-five, she refused to short-change herself.

"He knows I want the show to renew for another two years," she said. "Agreeing to this segment should seal the deal." The network exposure would bring more people to her restaurant back in Virginia, net her the money she wanted to expand her business and increase employment in Magnolia Falls. Plus, she had a plan to market her super-secret recipes for her specialty line of marinade sauces.

Expansion costs would be astronomical. But at twenty-nine and counting, she wanted to capitalize on this opportunity.

"I can't even imagine you acting remotely like a diva." Eric shook his head, the silver and black knitted cap he'd chosen to cover his bald head glittering in the ranch's lights. "You're no-nonsense, but generous to a fault."

Besides she'd been shrouded in the memory of her loss for over four years. She'd love Scott with all her heart, but when she'd married him right out of culinary school, she'd parked her dreams to create another one with him.

Slowly, she'd reclaimed bits and pieces of herself after the horrific crash that had stolen more than him from her. She pressed her palm against her belly and willed an old ache to subside before she made her way to the front desk.

*Focus on today and the future. There's nothing to gain from missing something you'll never have now.* "Speaking of no-nonsense, I'd like to check out the kitchen facilities after we check-in." She glanced around the expansive lobby, taking in the snowcapped mountains through the floor-to-ceiling windows. "Eagle Point Ranch is definitely decked out for the season." Logs crackled and sparked in a gargantuan fireplace festooned with garland and holiday decor, a cheerful display of reds, silvers, golds and greenery.

"Yeah, perfect for the shows we're filming here,"

Eric said.

"I wish we were taping them. These live shows are giving me mental hives." She suppressed an inner shudder. "I'm nervous about royally screwing up."

"You'll cover up any slips with your trademark sense of humor."

Her ability to laugh at her own mistakes had gotten her through the worst of the competition's moments. "Thanks," she said. "You going to track down our director while I tour the kitchen?"

"Angela's probably on the slopes since we don't start filming until Monday."

"And I have two glorious days to relax and enjoy a well-deserved break." Maybe she'd even hit the mountains too—the bunny beginner trails because she'd never tried to ski before.

Besides the instructors might be cute and, after putting her flirting skills on the back burner of her life, she was determined to reclaim that side of herself before she hit the big 3-0. Not that she wanted love and marriage again. But her female parts had been on a super long sabbatical and she missed being with someone, the thrill and the connection.

"I'll check us in, get our keycards. Go ahead and park here," she said to Eric, pointing to one of the groupings of chairs circling a rustic, low coffee table.

"I'll try to track down Bill while I wait," he said, sitting and unzipping his parka.

"Sounds good."

She swiveled around and instantly bumped into something hard and immoveable, and being the first kind of klutz, she slipped.

Powerful arms wrapped around her, steadying her before she hit the floor. "Sorry about that," a man's husky voice drawled as he released her from his strong, powerful grip. "Should have been watching where I was going. You okay?"

The scent of leather and man mingled with the wood smoke, and a ridiculous number of tingles traveled through her the second she found her footing and locked eyes with his. But then, it'd been a long time since she'd been held by a man, let alone one with Female Pheromone Magnet stamped on his handsome features.

She struggled to untangle her tongue and speak coherently while he gave her a crooked smile that only made him more appealing. He seemed to dwarf her with his broad shoulders and height, which, given her curvy, tallish figure, didn't happen often. She'd never win any awards for being petite or super skinny.

"I'm fine," Reagan said when her vocal cords finally cooperated with her muddled brainwaves.

He tipped his hand to his Stetson and those whiskey colored eyes of his glinted with a hint of amusement. "So, no permanent damage."

She smiled. Other than her long-neglected hormones zooming along her nerves, making her jittery as a mouse staring down a cat. A very hungry one.. But man, did she ever wish he'd take a bite of her. *Grab a hold of yourself.* Men like this tall, ridiculously gorgeous guy, didn't typically gravitate to women with her dress size.

"Nope. I'm good."

"Great. How about I make up for being such an oaf and buy you a drink later tonight as a way of apologizing?"

Brent Lancaster gave his new assignment another once over, waiting for her to stop twisting the wedding bands on her ring finger and answer his question. Normally, he'd never hit on a married woman, but he knew Reagan Harlow had been widowed years ago.

Damn shame.

Then, according to her brother, this hot number had focused on her career, stayed off the market for any and every possibility of hooking up permanently or short term again. Another damn shame. She had the lushest body he'd seen in a long time with curves begging for a man's caress.

But that wasn't why he'd asked her out. Or deliberately run into her just now. "Don't tell me you're already spoken for," he said, glancing down at her now wringing hands.

"I, uh, no," she stammered, turning the glittering diamond ring inward. "I've been alone for a long time. Just haven't..." her voice trailed off and she glanced down, then back up again. "I'm free, but."

"I'm Brent. Brent Lancaster." He introduced himself, cutting her off. "And you're?"

"Reagan Harlow," she said, taking the hand he offered and shaking it quickly.

"So how about it, Reagan?" he asked. "You going to give a guy a break and say yes? I may look tough, but I've got a fragile ego."

She laughed. The rich tone washed over him, warmed him in places he rarely examined since he'd left the Marines to join Covert Rescuers' Undercover Shield. "Well?" he asked.

"I'd hate to trample your feelings."

"So it's a date?"

"I, well. Yes. But I don't want to ditch my assistant." She looked at the man sitting in one of the chairs near them. "You have plans for tonight, Eric?"

The tall, slim man perked up and scooted to the edge of his seat. "Movies, totally chilling out in my room," he said. "Saving my strength for a day on the slopes tomorrow. Plus, I want to be on top of everything before we start filming the show on Monday."

"Show?" Brent asked though he already knew her reason for being at the luxury ranch. "Are you an actress?"

"No. Not even close," she said with sparkling eyes,

light dancing in the blue irises. "I host *Cooking Thyme* for the At Home Network. Speaking of that, I do have to check in and tour the kitchen, get a feel for the space."

He'd love to get a feel of her. But that wasn't on the agenda for this trip. His orders from the commander at CRUSH's headquarters in California hadn't included making the moves on Reagan. Just establish a rapport, safeguard her during the next two weeks without tipping her off, then return to San Francisco to begin his next covert mission.

Still, he'd been hired by her brother, not Reagan. And somehow that blurred the lines for him in ways he'd never expected to examine.

"Sure thing." He withdrew his cell phone. "Give me your number and I'll text you. That way we can find each other later."

"Sounds good."

She rattled off her number, he followed up, then said, "I'm glad I bumped into you. Going to make my vacation a lot more fun."

She flushed a pretty shade of pink, accentuating those amazing blue eyes, reminding him of the lake he swam in every summer while is father was stationed in Montana. "Ah, I. Okay then," she said. "Yes. Fun. Fun is good."

"Better check in, get your room sorted," he said. "Then we'll hook up. Say around six?"

"Six works."

"Excellent." He tucked his cell phone back in his pocket. "I'll reserve a table." Brent touched the Stetson's brim and tilted his head, then sauntered to the concierge's counter to make good on his promise.

And to keep a surreptitious watch on his voluptuous, sexy assignment.

She crossed the floor to the front desk, her fitted winter coat cinched in at the waist just above her lush, swaying ass which were her jeans molded to perfection. A zing of awareness charged through him, hit hard below his belt buckle. Hell. He grabbed a plastic cup from the table next to the concierge, filled it with the frou-frou citrus infused water from a hydration station and drank the entire glass.

The lemony-orange liquid cooled his throat, but his cock remained at granite levels. Damn. Guarding Reagan Harlow wouldn't be the cushy job he'd agreed to take on. He'd accepted the mission, figuring he'd have a mini vacation of sorts while helping out a guy who only wanted to protect his sister.

Sure, he'd known she was pretty in that all-American girl-next-door way when he'd studied her pictures, but he hadn't been prepared for the sensual wallop her body delivered. Spending time with her wouldn't be difficult. Keeping his paws off? Another problem altogether.

He diverted his instant attraction, focused his energy on reserving the table for two with his platinum credit card. One issued by his agency for off-the-grid missions.

Brent doubted Colton Sutler would be okay with his current state of arousal, but he'd control the urge to take this date to the next level. God knew, he could relate to the man's concern. He'd run interference on occasion with his own sisters, both of them now settled down with their own kids to raise, careers to pursue.

After slipping his wallet back into his leather jacket's inner pocket, Brent skimmed the concealed holster to remind himself to stand down. But man, he didn't want to stand down at all. Again, the devil on his shoulder nudged him to ignore his internal hallway sex monitor.

Reagan and her assistant parted company. Eric making his way to the hallway leading to the block of rooms in the main ranch while she'd been given a luxury cabin conveniently located next to his. By design. But she'd never know the truth.

Two weeks from now he'd be out of here and Reagan's show would resume filming in Magnolia Falls, Virginia where the people at the primary head-quarters for his agency had complete control over keeping her safe.

She made her way to the lobby doors and exited, then he slowly moved in the same direction, noting nothing out of the ordinary per his expectations. But before he stepped outside, he heard her scream.

# CHAPTER 2

ADRENALINE PUMPED THROUGH HIS VEINS, making his fingertips tingle as he rushed through the doors. "Reagan." Brent raced to where she lay sprawled in a snowbank next to her SUV, dropped beside her. "Are you okay?" He cruised his large hands over her body, checking for injuries.

"Yes. I'm fine," she said, struggling to stand. "Only my pride's bruised."

He helped her up. "What happened?" His heart rate slowed to a normal beat.

"I slipped on a patch of ice." She pointed to the offending strip of frozen water. "Which is so weird. Because I didn't see it before I checked in."

Neither did he, but he didn't voice his thoughts. "The hazards of winter," he said easily before kneeling back down to examine area and scraping a bit of ice to sniff it. The sweet, sugary scent eased his concern. "Spilled soda from what I can tell. With these subzero temps, wouldn't take long to freeze over."

Brent stood, then glanced to the empty parking spot next to hers. A fresh set of tire tracks were next to her SUV. He'd take an impression later, run a trace. Might be good to contact Hank Patterson too. Extra manpower from the former SEAL's elite group of Brotherhood Protectors could come in handy if this incident wasn't accidental.

"Well, that mystery's solved," Reagan said, brushing the remaining snow from her behind. "Thanks for coming to my rescue."

"Never know, this could become a thing," he said. "Not that I'd mind."

The frigid wind picked up the strands of her honey blonde hair, whipped them across her sun-kissed face. "I won't need pseudo bodyguard, but I am looking forward to seeing you later today." She brought out her key fob and unlocked her door. "It's been too long since I've gone on a date."

A heavy sensation banded around his chest. He hated hiding the original reason he had for being with her. She deserved a solid chance at another relationship, but he'd signed on for this mission and he'd stick to the protocol. "That's hard to believe," he said, shoving his hands in his coat pocket. "I'd expect loads of guys lining up for the chance to get to know you better." He meant the words, but a part of him wanted to cross the self-imposed professional line he stood by whenever working an assignment.

She stepped into the SUV, leaned toward him. "Pretty much all the guys I know back home are spoken for or totally not my type," Reagan said. "Plus, I'm way too busy pursuing my career to settle down again, Brent. Dinner, drinks, a little conversation with hot guy. That's what I am interested in, nothing more."

Her scent, a mix of spice and sugar, mingled with the crisp, winter air carrying the pine aromas in from the snowcapped mountains. His mouth watered for a taste of her. "Then we're on the same page," he said easily. "My company's eating up a lot of my time these days too." That much was true.

"Great." She flashed him another one of those bright smiles. "Keeps things easy. Nothing worse than raising false expectations."

Reagan closed the door and started the engine, then waved as he stepped back to give her room to back out and drive away.

He waited until the SUV's rear end faded from view, then knelt by the tire tracks next to her empty parking spot. After taking several scans with his cell phone and sending them to headquarters for analysis, he made his way to his tricked out black Toyota Tacoma truck. Then he rode to his cabin located next to hers, one he'd already beefed up with extra security.

He'd use the hours between now and their date to monitor the exterior of her cabin. The itinerary he'd gotten for her show's filming schedule and the final live run included filming at one of the local eateries. Al's Diner with its world famous burgers would add local flair to the show, bring in curious tourists then and later.

Crowds. Never a good thing when trying to protect a client who'd hired his agency's services. But one who didn't have a clue? Even harder. But not impossible. The word didn't even belong in his vocabulary.

He checked the computer monitor which showed all exterior views of the cabin next to his along with interior cams revealing her movements inside the spacious living room. She'd removed her form-fitting winter parka and boots, her roller bag lay open on the bed in a separate space.

Now she sat in the plush sofa in front of the fireplace making notes on her laptop with a swath of papers next to her.

The woman didn't mess around. She didn't waste a single second, staying focused on her tasks. But then Reagan twisted her rings on her finger, murmured something under her breath. Finally, she removed them, set them on the table next to her.

She returned her attention to the laptop, lifted a few papers, made notations. He could even see the tiny line between her brows. Then, suddenly, Reagan lowered her head, brought her hands to her face, shoulders heaving.

Seconds later, she swiped her eyes and picked up the wedding bands to slide them back onto her ring finger. Then she resumed her work with renewed vigor, mumbling words of self-encouragement to herself.

Brent shuttered his gaze for a moment. A heavy feeling dropped low in his belly, then knotted. He hated that she cried alone. He hated that she couldn't truly move forward. Not when grief still haunted her.

Despite her assertion earlier, he wanted more than a few fake dates with this strong woman who'd overcome a major loss. And, the words she'd spoken hadn't fooled him. She didn't want more than a few friendly hookups—he'd heard the vulnerability in her voice.

Then, just now, witnessing her struggle, made him want to do more than kiss her senseless. Her loneliness, masked by smiles and a passion to create something more for herself, made him want to take her into his arms. He wanted hold her, let her know she could have so much more if she'd give someone a chance to get truly close to her.

Someone who didn't throw himself into the line of fire on a regular basis. Because the last person his gorgeous client needed in her life was a guy like him. She'd already gone through too much. He'd guard her, physically. Play the role he'd been assigned and then move on.

REAGAN'S CELL PHONE CHIMED, interrupting her workflow. She picked it up and read the screen, then replied to Eric to confirm her tour of the ranch's kitchen facilities and meet the head chef. After rifling through her clothes, she selected another comfy pair of jeans, a T-shirt with her show's logo emblazoned over the top left side and a crimson cardigan.

Her former competitor, Owen Davidson, had checked in and had toured the facility. The forty-five-year-old had agreed to a reunion one year after she'd fought him in the finals and won the coveted show hosting slot.

While driving back to the ranch's main building— more like a luxury resort—she reminisced about their battles in the kitchen. Reagan had thought for sure he'd win. After all, Owen came from a long line of restauranteurs in New York City's Manhattan district. The dishes he'd prepared during the competition's shows had been intricate, elaborate and beyond delicious.

But difficult to replicate in someone's home, especially if their budgets didn't include money for high end ingredients.

By the time she reached the ranch, the afternoon

sun had begun its descent toward the horizon, casting a glare on her windshield. Grabbing her satchel which held her laptop and recipes, she gave herself a cursory glance in the rearview mirror before she stepped back out into the frigid Montana air. Within minutes, she and Eric hooked up with her director.

"Where's Owen?" Reagan asked.

Angela Romera sifted through the paperwork she'd brought with her. "He said something about taking advantage of the hot tub at his cabin with his current date." She pushed her square-shaped glasses up her nose and pursed her full lips. "I went over the scripts and recipes for the shows we're filming with him. He's got a few of his signature holiday recipes queued up."

"I'll go coordinate with him, make sure we didn't let anything slip through the cracks before I tour the kitchen. I want to make sure the restaurant's staff knows about everything we'll need to set up shop." Reagan had been exchanging ideas with the chef for several months in anticipation of their reunion shows. They'd finalized most of the details, but Owen had a way of throwing in curve balls at the last minute. "Don't want to leave anything to chance." She'd already suffered through a major life hijacking, one she'd carried a burden of guilt about for years. The loss of her husband and her pregnancy had rippled her heart to shreds. Only her work, her escape into the kitchen, had brought a measure of peace.

"Good thinking," Angela said. "Eric, his shipment of supplies is coming in later today from Bozeman. Keep an eye out for it and make sure to get them to Owen as soon as they arrive."

Eric nodded, tapped a note into his tablet. "Got it. I'll go into Eagle Rock on Monday morning to coordinate the filming with Al at his diner."

"Sounds good," Angela said, then straightened and locked her amber eyes onto Reagan's. "The sleigh ride segment depends on cooperative weather, but if we need to switch venues, I know you'll handle the change beautifully."

Reagan smiled. Her director's confidence in her brought a wash of warmth through her body. Angela Romera's stellar reputation in the industry had been honed through rising up the ranks of home television networks from production assistant to producer to director.

All while raising three, equally as intelligent and driven daughters and celebrating thirty-five years of marriage earlier that year.

"I've got a homemade marshmallow s'more with a kick of amaretto in the hot chocolate for the fireside gathering regardless of what happens on Wednesday," she said. "The ranch has a great area around the fireplace to gather if necessary."

"Good thinking," Angela said. "Right. So the

schedule as it stands is first reunion show on Monday afternoon here in the ranch's kitchen, White Oak Ranch for a cookie bake off with Sadie McClain and her family on Tuesday, then the sleigh ride on Wednesday. Al's Diner on Thursday, Christmas dinner with all the fixings on the actual day, then a few well-deserved days off until we wrap up on New Year's Eve."

"Spending the winter holidays in Montana," Reagan said. "What could be more idyllic?"

"Christmas in the Caribbean," Eric said wryly, then slipped his tablet into his crossbody man purse. "I'll check the best lighting options for the camera crew when I meet with Al as well as for all the other shows so we can hit the ground running on Monday."

"Perfect. Touch base with me afterward," Angela said. "Now I'm off to find my guy, see if he wants to grab an early dinner before we take advantage of our hot tub. Owen can't be the only one on this team having fun while we're here."

*Fun.* The word ricocheted through her brain, brought a renewed rush of anticipation as Reagan thought about her date with Brent Lancaster later that day. Her face flushed hot and she swallowed hard.

Twisting her rings round and round, she swallowed hard, fought to cool the heat blazing through her veins.

"Hello? Earth to Reagan."

Eric's voice brought her out of momentary daze. "Sorry, what?" she asked.

"I just wondered what you had planned for tonight," Angela said.

"Oh, I, uh." Reagan clasped her hands, looked down at her boots, then back at Angela. "Well..." The rings she'd fisted dug into her palm. Rings she'd worn to remind her on a daily basis that the man who'd given them to her had died so she could live.

Eric laughed. "Don't worry about your star. She's actually got a date tonight."

Angela arched an eyebrow, then gazed at the bands on Reagan's finger. "Don't you think it's time to take them off?" she asked gently.

Reagan released her grip on her hands, let them drop to her sides, felt the weight of guilt tugging down her shoulders as if she held ten pound barbells. She'd tried. Oh, how she'd tried. Moving on meant letting go of her past. Of the guilt. And she had moved on in so many ways, but still, Scott had been her first love and setting the bands aside meant stepping into extremely unfamiliar territory.

She wet her lips, inhaled a deep breath. "It's just drinks. No big deal. And he knows I'm available." But her husband had been inextricably linked to her for years before they'd realized more than friendship existed between them.

"I don't know, Reagan," Eric said. "The way Mr.

Tall, Hot and Stetson looked at you didn't scream *no big deal.*"

"Good." Angela touched Reagan's shoulder and squeezed, offering her comfort and a bit of encouragement in her frank gaze. "Just don't get too distracted. I need you on top of your game during the next two weeks."

"You've got nothing to worry about," Reagan said. "This guy's just being nice, that's all. I'm not even close to being in his league." But that didn't mean she wouldn't give her rusty dating skills a polish before meeting Brent Lancaster.

And maybe, just maybe, he'd be the right kind of guy to bridge the divide between all her yesterdays with the future she wanted to carve out.

With that thought in mind, she said goodbye to everyone, completed her tour of the kitchen with the ranch's sous chef, checked the fridges and freezers to make sure all her supplies had arrived on time. Then she made her way back to her rental, telling herself she'd pull out all the stops for Mr. Tall, Hot and Stetson.

By five-fifty-five, after trying and discarding multiple outfits for her *no big deal* date, she found the perfect combo of dressy and casual. Then, checking her cell when Brent texted her, she struggled to push down the lump forming in her throat, telling herself again she'd mourned long enough and one date didn't mean a betrayal, only a slice of a new beginning with no commitments or future involvements required. Heaving a deep breath, she carefully removed her rings and slipped them into her traveling jewelry bag.

The pang she expected to hit her again didn't jab behind her sternum. Instead, a tingling sensation radiated through her body, skipped along her nerves, making every cell vibrate with anticipation.

CHAPTER 3

"I'm sure her brother's overreacting, but I get it," Brent said to Hank Patterson after touching base with Reagan about their date. He'd pick her up in less than fifteen minutes. "I'd appreciate if you had a few of your guys at the ranch on Tuesday for *Cooking Thyme's* filming. More as a precaution."

"No problems with the tire tracks?"

"None." Brent read the report his team had sent back to him once more. "The tracks belonged to a Subaru driven by a family visiting the area for a ski vacation. Most likely, one of their kids accidentally spilled the soda."

"Spills come with the territory when you've got kids."

"You speak from experience."

"Emma's a sweetheart, but toddlers are messy."

Brent smiled. The former SEAL couldn't hide the love in his voice. Lucky guy, but Brent had learned the hard way not to count on luck in the love department.

They ended their call, then he slipped on his holster and shrugged on his leather jacket to conceal the weapon he carried. Stepping outside, he noted the empty road, lights flickering in the cabins surrounding his and Reagan's place.

Laughter, the sound of hot tubs bubbling echoed in the frosty air. Clattering on decks and the smell of wood smoke mingled with the fresh mountain pine scent. The moon had already begun its climb into the darkening sky.

Eagle Point Ranch's 5 Star accommodations offered a perfect winter holiday getaway vacation.

A motor gunned in the distance while he strode over packed snow to his SUV. He turned in the sound's direction. Snow mobiles riding out on the trails leading to various hideaways dotting the ranch's property.

Nothing to investigate. Just people having a good time on their way to more of the same.

Too bad this date he'd engineered with Reagan wouldn't lead to a similar outcome. Because the memory of her lush body and gorgeous face had given him all kinds of can't-keep-his-hands-off thoughts.

Thoughts that slammed him below the belt the minute she answered her cabin door. She'd refreshed her makeup just enough to make those blue eyes sparkle like sapphires and her plump lips even more kissable with the pale pink gloss she'd painted on them.

"You're early," she said, welcoming him inside. "Make yourself comfortable while I get my purse and coat." She indicated the sofa in front of the fireplace.

He followed her gesture. Her left hand glaringly bare of the wedding bands. His breath stalled. Damn. He'd have to move with caution, but the playbook for this date just got a lot more complicated.

"Take your time," he said, drinking in the sight of the way the tunic top's bright turquoise and fuchsia pattern accentuated her creamy skin and honey-blonde hair which curled in waves down one side of her oval shaped face. "You look nice." Nice? More like gorgeous.

She blinked, then looked down while brushing her palms down the distressed, casual jeans which molded to her curves in all the right ways. "Thanks. I had no idea what to wear, but I figure the ranch's restaurant isn't super formal. I mean, it's Montana. In winter."

"Those boots don't look like they'd survive a hike in the woods," he said, giving her a steady gaze then moving it lower to the high, soft black boots rising to just above her knee.

Boots that were meant more for style than function. Though he could think of plenty other ways to utilize them.

The sexy, fuck-me boots and the double-wrapped roped choker with the shining pendant at the base of her throat gave him all kinds of flashes of fantasies.

Of the naked kind.

She licked her lips, flushing prettily to that rose color he'd like to find in other places. "Oh, yeah. Well, yes. They're not. But sometimes you've got to suffer to be beautiful." Reagan gave him a sassy grin before lifting her form-fitting winter coat from the stand next to the door. She picked up her purse and then she nibbled her that delectable lower lip.

Oh, yeah. Things got way more complicated. Her nerves, coupled with the sass despite them, only made him want to gather her into his arms, kiss her. Do a whole lot more. And skip the drinks, dinner for another kind of date altogether.

Fuck. *Stand down. Remember why you're here.* But another voice, the devil riding his shoulder ever since he escaped his strict military father's fists, whispered... *technically, she didn't hire you.*

"Here, let me help you with that," he said, turning on the charm and slipping the coat over her shoulders, waiting until she had her arms safely inside. Then he turned her round and pulled up the zipper until he reached the base of her throat where the pendant sat, teasing him.

*This gig is just a precaution. There's no credible threat against her. Just one over-protective brother asking for top cover. Why not act on the attraction pinging between us if tonight leads somewhere? We're adults.*

They'd part ways after New Year's Eve, and no one would be the wiser. Right?

Wrong. Really wrong. But still. The cobalt darkening her blue eyes made not taking this charade to the next level an even more idiotic idea.

After all, he couldn't back off now without sending her an even worse message. That he didn't want her. A gargantuan lie.

But he'd better make damn sure she never learned the truth.

REAGAN HAD THOUGHT Brent would rush through the drinks, go through the motions during their dinner. After all, what would they have in common other than being in the same place at the same time?

But he'd surprised her. They'd lingered over signature cocktails, chatting easily while taking their time to order appetizers and their main courses.

"Sounds like your sisters gave you a run for your money," she said after he poured her another glass of wine.

"Twins. Double trouble as far as I'm concerned."

"I bet my brother's glad there aren't two of me," she said, laughing.

The corners next to Brent's whiskey eyes crinkled. "Most likely he'd have at least a few gray hairs before turning thirty. As it is, my sisters each have two rugrats a piece and those kids are giving them serious payback. But family, taking care of each other, growing together is the fun part of life. I want that one day."

His voice revealed so much genuine love, affection, that she had to suppress another long held ache. But she didn't reveal the truth. No point. This was just a conversation, not a lifetime commitment.

"That's great," she said, knowing now, without a shadow of doubt, that she'd never take this dating or holiday fling beyond the time they had here.

"What about your brother? He settling down now?"

"Yeah," she said easily, sipping her cabernet. "He's going to become a father soon. That'll keep him too occupied to continue all his long-distance hovering." She'd finally checked in with him earlier that day and learned about her sister-in-law's pregnancy.

Her throat closed. She swallowed hard, pushed down the old hurt with a stern reminder. *This is a date*. A simple dinner and drink getting-to-know-you evening didn't have space for sad stories about losses too incomprehensible to share.

Brent reached across the table and covered her left hand with his, stroked his thumb pad over her knuckles "What are your plans for tomorrow?" he asked softly.

His featherlight caress spiraled heat beneath her skin, fuzzed her ability to think clearly. How long had she lived without a tender gesture, one that could lead to more or be just enough in that moment? She let the sensation, the connection ground her before picking up her fork to spear another bite of exquisitely roasted vegetables. "Sleeping in, then I set up a ski lesson on the bunny slope at noon," she said after taking a bite. "Hopefully, I won't make a total fool of myself, but if a tiny patch of ice can drop me on my ass, anything's possible. How about you?"

"Bunny slope is a definite no, but I'll be out there." He draped one arm over the free chair next to him as he glanced outside. "Good powder out there now."

Light snowflakes floated down to the hills, valley and mountains beyond, coating the surrounding trees with a blanket of glistening white. "Sounds like you've got experience."

"Grew up on a military base near Bozeman." His tilted his head to the side and a small smile played on his lips. "Spent most of my teen years on the slopes or in the lake during the summer."

That thumb continued moving over her skin, tracing lazy circles, igniting all kinds of sparks. She locked eyes with his. Streaks of darker brown striated through the whiskey-colored irises. A long neglected feminine pride resurrected. He wanted her. Her!

Something else unfurled low, traveled into her breasts, making them full, heavy. "I don't suppose you'd consider trading the black diamond trail for the bunny slope?" she asked. "You know. To make sure I don't injure myself. After all, you've come to my rescue twice." She lifted her last bite to her mouth, watched his eyes track their way to her lips and every hormone she possessed zinged all the way to her nipples, tightening them.

He grinned, continued the nerve tingling stroking over her skin, the movements branding her with heat. "You probably do need someone to protect your..." he turned her hand into his, linked fingers with hers. "Assets."

He drawled out the last word, but there was nothing slow and easy in the promise gleaming in his answering gaze. Her pulse skittered wildly in her throat. So wildly she thought the accelerating beat could bounce the pendant resting there. "Yes. My assets definitely need someone to watch over them. I'd hate to show up on the live set with a broken bone. Wouldn't be good."

"Hmmm," he said. "I agree. Wouldn't be good at all. Plus, I've got a vested interest in keeping those bones and everything else about you intact."

"Oh?" she asked, sinking deeper into the mesmerizing way he touched her, held her eyes locked with his. "Why?"

"I happen to like the way they're packaged."

"Well, is it a date then?"

"Oh, honey, it's definitely a date." He waved over the server, got their dinner plates cleared. "Got any room left room for dessert?"

"The flourless chocolate torte with the raspberry coulis is amazing," their server suggested eagerly, offering a Reagan a menu with several selections.

Her heartbeat accelerated, her gaze still on Brent's instead of focusing on the restaurant's premiere offerings. Right now, the only dessert she was interested sat across from her with sexy, dangerously hot gleaming eyes and a mouth she wanted to nibble on. She blinked. Her brain had definitely snapped out of female hibernation and into full-on go for the entire package.

"You're the expert," Brent said. "What do you recommend?"

Quickly, she forced herself to look at the different items the restaurant offered while inhaling a deep breath in a last ditch attempt to control her reaction to him. The letters jumbled and her ability to concentrate evaporated, but she recalled her tour earlier that day along with the head chef's suggestions for one of their shows the following week.

"We'll go with the torte and I'd like to try the warm bread pudding with vanilla sauce," she said decisively. After all, no matter how much she wanted the man *that way* she'd slow things down just a bit.

Sure. She hadn't been a complete nun during the years she'd been widowed, but Reagan didn't jump into the sack with just anyone no matter how much her hormones screamed for her to go, go, go for it. Still, she'd never had this intense a reaction to a man since she'd fallen for her high school sweetheart.

And after the dessert arrived, the succulent flavors dancing on her tongue couldn't compete with her craving for a taste of Mr. Tall, Hot and Stetson.

BRENT WALKED Reagan to her cabin door, the light snow falling around them, landing on her blonde hair, dusting it like spun sugar. "I had a good time tonight," he said, meaning every word. Who cared what had brought them together? Maybe this could turn out way different than he'd expected when he'd accepted this off-the-grid assignment.

"Me, too." She brought out her keycard, but didn't turn away from him, clasping it in her gloved hand. "So tomorrow? Still game for skiing with a total beginner?"

"Absolutely."

"Sooooo." She held his gaze, her breath misting the air. "I should go in."

"Yeah, wouldn't want you to freeze." He wanted to close the scant distance between them, hold her and brush the snowflakes from her cheeks, kiss the luscious pink lips frosted with the same soft snow. Then take the keycard and let them both inside to act on the promise sparking in her blue eyes throughout their date. And now. "But I can think of a few ways to warm you up."

"I bet you can, but…"

"Hey, no pressure." He framed her cheeks and caressed her rosy cheeks with his thumbs. "We'll take this slow and easy." In the distance, a wolf howled, and the sound of tires crunching on the road behind them cut through the winter quiet night.

"Slow and easy sounds good," she said. "But not too slow." Reagan nibbled her lower lip, then stepped a smidge closer to him and moved her mouth over his briefly before breaking the contact.

"Good night, Brent." She waved the keycard over the door lock and walked inside. Then, standing in the soft glow of the floor lamp by the window, she smiled shyly. "Pick me up at ten?"

The smile. God. How did a simple, shy smile make him want to protect her as a man, not a hired bodyguard? "Ten works," he said. "See you tomorrow, Reagan. And be sure to lock up."

"Those overprotective brother instincts kicking in?"

He laughed. "You asked me to watch over you, remember? Like I said, I've got a vested interested in protecting your assets."

She leaned against the doorjamb, slightly closing the door, held his gaze. "Then I'll lock up and double bolt it too." Then she moved into the room and shut the door slowly.

Brent waited until he heard the locks click into place, then made his way down the stairs to his SUV, the taste of her lingering on his mouth, tingled on his lips. The light kiss, so sweet, tender even, tasted just like he'd expected. Vanilla, hints of raspberry and chocolate, mingling with her unique essence. Damn. Though everything in him had wanted to nudge her to the next level, the man he'd been before becoming a covert agent managed to rein him in.

After driving the short distance between their cabins and entering his, he tossed the keycard onto a side table and shrugged off his jacket. Still wearing his holster, he went to the kitchen, drew out a cold beer and popped the cap, took a healthy swallow.

He drank the brew slowly while checking his monitors, watching over her per his orders. But also out of ingrained years of service to his family, his mother and sisters. Watching her move into the bedroom adjacent to the main living area, he brought his fingers to his still tingling lips.

God. How long had it been since he'd just been with someone, gotten to truly know her? He'd forgotten the thrill of the chase, the drawn out seduction playing like a ballad instead of rushing headlong into adrenaline induced sex.

Reagan deserved the ballad, the slow dance.

And, maybe, he did too.

# CHAPTER 4

"Okay, I think there's a reason I never learned to ski," Reagan said ruefully, her butt good and frozen after the umpteenth fall on the bunny slope. "Clearly, I lack the coordination to navigate ice and snow." After two hours on the mountain, she'd been on the ground more than moving over the powder fresh snow that had fallen the night before.

The clouds had given way to a clear, blue sky. In the distance, far better skiers flew down the more challenging trails. Trails she knew Brent itched to go down, but true to his word, he'd stuck with her all morning.

"Here," he said, grinning and holding out his hand. "Let me help you up."

"Why?" She pouted a bit. "I'll only fall again."

"I'll hold you steady until we get back down to the base."

She adjusted her goggles. "Fine, but once we're back, I want you to take advantage of this…" Reagan slid a ski over the snow. "Perfect powder. I'd feel awful if you didn't get a few runs in. You came here to ski, not hang out on the bunny slope"

"Sure, but I happen to like the ski bunny I'm with right now."

"I'm no ski bunny, more like a ski tortoise." Everything about skiing made her feel awkward, all klutz and uncomfortable in the ski bib and pants. A sausage in winter wear. "Please do what you planned to do when you got here, Brent. I don't want to ruin your vacation."

He held out his hand again. "My plans changed after I met you," he said. "Now come on. Let's get off this mountain, head back to the ranch and warm up by the fire, grab a bite to eat."

Her stomach grumbled in answer to his offer. "You're sure?" She let him pull her up again and wobbled once more on her skis.

"Yes." He brought her in front of his broad chest. "Make a V with your skis and take it slow. Don't stiffen up. Relax."

*Relax?* Kind of hard to do when now her knees wobbled for very different reasons than the slippery slope. "Okay," she said, glancing down the small hill toward the base. "It's not that far. I can make it there in one piece." Even if she had to skid down on her poor, sore as hell ass.

Brent matched her pace, skiing easily nearby her. "Almost there," he said, encouraging her.

A little girl whipped past her, edging around them with more expertise in her tiny body than Reagan could possibly hope to possess. Then another kid shot ahead as she struggled to remain upright.

"You've got this," Brent said.

"Says the Black Diamond trail expert," she muttered, but she doggedly persisted, half-skiing and bumbling to the bottom where another group of grade school children listen to their instructor.

She leaned on her poles, huffed a satisfied breath. "I did it." Maybe not with grace. But still, another life goal to tick off her personal bucket list.

"You want to go again when you get a break from filming the show next week?" Brent used one of his poles to pop his boots free of his skis, then released hers.

"Uh, no." She kneeled to pick up her skis at the same time he did. "I think my skiing days are over. I'm putting this in the one and done category along with the 5K race I ran in October."

"Not into sports?" Brent asked when they both stood, holding their rentals.

She walked beside him, her heavy ski boots ridiculously clunky. "I worked the snack stand in high school, but no. Not so much." Athleticism wasn't her deal, though she had been in the stands cheering for the Magnolia Falls' high school football team every Friday. Cheering for her brother and his friends, including Scott.

She mentally pocketed the memories, mementoes that brought a measure of happiness. Ones she cherished. But today? Today she wanted to make new memories, however fleeting.

With Brent.

They made their way back to the ski shop, returned their rentals and Brent took her by the hand, walking easily beside her toward the full parking lot. A silver SUV entered it, honking, hurtling toward them.

"Watch out." Brent moved her between two parked vehicles, shielding her, barricading her body with his. "They've lost control of their car."

She froze, temporarily rooted to the spot, unable to move. The hairs on the back of her neck raised and sweat beaded above her lip. Another memory flashed, and she tasted acid. Metal coated the back of her throat. The SUV skidded, fishtailed left and smashed into oversized red truck's cargo bed, then shuddered to a stop.

Air bags deployed, filling the windshield but not before she caught sight of the driver and his passenger. "Oh my god," she cried, struggling to get around Brent, who held her back with his outstretched arm. "Let me go. Please. They could be hurt."

"They could've hit you," he grunted, still barring her from rushing to them.

"Not on purpose. I know them." She shoved around him and raced to the SUV. "Call for help."

"Eric. Angela," she called as she reached the SUV and pulled the driver's side door handle. "Are you okay? Please tell me you're okay." She'd already lost someone she loved deeply to a horrific car crash. Her family was far flung all over the world. Her friends had become a second one to her.

No way would she lose them too. And no way would she let Brent Lancaster treat her like a hothouse flower when she'd become stronger than she'd ever thought possible in the aftermath of the accident that had stolen dreams she didn't dare dream for again.

BRENT RUSHED AFTER REAGAN, determined to stop her in her tracks, but when she called her co-workers' names, the adrenaline propelling him to her eased up. Groans, coughing and sputters filled the air.

A crowd began to gather, lolly gaggling at the scene with morbid curiosity. "Stand back," he cautioned, then turned to a guy standing close by. "Call 911."

The twenty-something skier nodded and brought out his mobile. "On it."

"They're okay," Reagan said when he reached her. "Just shook up."

Eric moaned. "Sorry. I hit a patch of ice, lost control.

Brent released the man's seatbelt. "You're lucky you didn't do worse damage. Good thing you warned us with the horn."

The airbags had done their job, protecting the passengers but now the white dust coated everything inside, including Eric and Angela who had already unbuckled her belt and opened her door. "We're supposed to meet Owen and his girlfriend at the ski shop," she said haltingly. "Need to text…" her voice stuttered to a stop as her eyes rolled back.

Shit. "Reagan. Stay with Eric." He circled the rear end and got to Angela's side in seconds. After checking her pulse, still strong, he inventoried the rest of her injuries. Bruises colored her forehead and right cheek. "She might be concussed. We'll let the emergency crew handle moving her just in case there's more going on internally."

"God. This is all my fault," Eric groaned. "What if she can't direct tomorrow?"

"*Cooking Thyme* is the least of our concerns right now," Reagan said, then shot Brent a worried look. "I have no idea how long it'll take the local emergency services to get here."

"Ski Patrol can fill the gap," he assured her while pushing the deployed airbag out of Angela's way.

God. He hated seeing the haunted look in her eyes when only minutes ago they'd been sparkling, happy. "I'm sure she's fine."

"We won't know that until she's checked out thoroughly." Reagan jerked out her cell phone, removed her gloves, then texted. "I'm giving her husband and Owen the heads up."

The wail of a distant siren cut through the murmuring crowd and the whirr of a snow mobiles joined the response. Relief flooded him as the EMTs, and patrol arrived on the scene. The team of emergency workers quickly triaged Angela and Eric.

Leaving them to do their jobs, he went to Reagan who had moved to the sidelines. "How you holding up?" he asked.

Her lips chattered. "I'm okay," she said. "Angela's husband's going straight to the Urgent Care clinic in Eagle Rock. Owen's on his back to the main ranch lodge building. We're supposed to meet with the rest of the show's crew in an hour."

Brent pulled her into his embrace, warming her with his body, wishing he could erase the lines furrowing her forehead. "I'll take you there now." He stroked her back, running his hands up and down the ski jacket. "Should give us time to grab a quick bite first."

"Thanks," she said, wrapping her arms around his waist. "Sorry the rest of our date is over."

She trembled slightly, and he held her tighter,

lowering his forehead to hers. "Not your fault," he said gently. "Let's get you out of this cold before we both turn into popsicles."

"I just hope she's okay."

Her breath misted the air between them as her blue eyes locked onto his. "They're just erring on the side of caution."

"It's just. I…" she broke off, lowered her gaze.

The catch in her voice lanced him behind the sternum. Today's accident had resurrected the memory of her devastating loss. "You what?" he asked, already knowing the answer, but unable to reveal the fact.

"I know what happened today is different, but I survived a car accident that killed my husband. His internal injuries were too devastating to save him," she said, her eyes shining with unshed tears. "Not exactly date conversation, but… sorry." She buried her head into the shelter of his shoulder.

"Hey." He kissed the top of her head. "You don't have to hide how you feel, your past, from me. I figured you must have had someone special when I first saw the bands." And she'd taken them off for him before their first date the night before.

She slowly released him, stepped back. "They're part of who I am," she said. "What I had, the love I shared with him, didn't die that day, but I'm a different person now."

"I happen to like that person a lot," he said. "I

enjoyed last night. Today too." That wasn't a lie, despite the fact he'd had to hide his real reason for being in Montana from her.

He cocked his head to his SUV, the sound of the emergency crew's sirens fading in the crisp, winter air. "How about we head back now? I heard the grilled cheese the ranch serves up is the best." Hell, he wanted to do more than share a few drinks and meals with her. But connecting with Reagan, acting on the heat flaring between them from the minute he'd caught her mid-fall, meant lowering some of his guard too.

Later. For now, he'd focus on taking her mind off her past and get her thinking squarely about the future, even if a lasting one with him wasn't in the cards.

She smiled. "I gave them my recipe. So I know it's the best."

Warmth spread through him, filled his chest, flowed through his veins. Damn. The girl had spirit. He took her hand and they made their way across the lane toward his SUV. "Then I definitely want to try it," he said, opening her door to let her inside.

"I overreacted when you tried to hold me back from the wreck," she said after he stepped into the driver's side. "Boy, you moved fast. Felt like you've got firsthand experience in this rescuing business."

Shit. Her brother had been a DEA agent before moving to Italy to oversee the installation of another CRUSH headquarters. "I'm a Marine," he admitted.

"You're on leave? I thought you were a businessman or something."

"You're not far off the mark. I left a few years ago after my third tour of duty," he said, giving her just enough of the truth that'd also cover his ass. "My company provides discrete security services. We've got contracts and clients all over the country, but my offices are located north of San Francisco."

"Sort of like Sadie Patterson's husband?"

"You could say that." Only, his work usually meant running dangerous missions all over the world.

If she discovered the reason he'd shown up in Montana, she might never forgive him. But he didn't plan on letting her discover the truth. Not unless he couldn't avoid it.

Today's near miss had been a close call, but unless he learned otherwise from the sheriff's report, he'd continue to tread the path he'd chosen.

## CHAPTER 5

REAGAN CLUTCHED her bag of ingredients in one hand while waving goodbye to Owen, who'd driven her back to her cabin. Within seconds, she'd entered her cozy cabin. After stamping the snow off her boots, she carried everything she'd gotten from Eagle Point's restaurant staff into the efficiently supplied kitchen to unload them.

Her cell phone vibrated in her back pocket. She withdrew it, smiled at the text from Brent.

**Do you need me to bring anything?**

**Just your appetite.**

**Always with me.**

She read his response, laughed. The man had a healthy appetite. Hours earlier, they'd noshed on grilled cheese sandwiches filled with creamy, melted sharp cheddar mixed with savory, caramelize onions complemented with a lush tomato-basil bisque.

He'd walked with her to the ranch's kitchens where she connected with *Cooking Thyme's* staff, then left her to take advantage of the remaining free hours to ski the black diamond slopes. After the meeting, she'd gone to the chef and asked for the ingredients to make a dinner any red-blooded man would wolf down.

Nothing like a thick, juicy steak cooked to perfection by reverse searing it. Within a half an hour, a pair of thick beef tenderloins baked at a low temp in the oven and a simple salad had been tossed, waiting for a dash of light, homemade balsamic vinaigrette. Small potatoes had been parboiled, ready to roast after she pulled the steaks out to sear them right before serving.

Reagan made her way to the cabin's bedroom suite for a well-deserved shower. Afterward, with a towel wrapped around her wet hair and another tucked around her body, she rifled through her drawers, looking for something way sexier than the serviceable underwear and bras she'd packed for this trip.

But then, things might not go that far anyway.

Still, she made a mental note to hit the local lingerie shop and buy stuff that'd make her feel feminine, attractive... seductive... from here on out. Because no matter where things went with Brent, she planned on having a life that extended beyond her pots and pans in the future.

With that thought in mind, she grabbed the least boring pair of panties she'd brought with her and started to dress.

A bell chimed just as she finished applying her makeup. Her heart rate ramped up and she took one more cursory look in the mirror, added another layer of gloss to her mouth, then blew herself a kiss.

An old high school habit she'd developed to give herself female confidence, courage.

Heck, if she didn't love herself, accept who she was flaws and all, then who would?

She twirled away from the mirror, went to the door and opened it, smiling, expecting to see Brent. "You're a bit earl...," she stopped, her stomach hollowing out when she saw Eric standing there instead. "What's wrong? Is it Angela?"

His pale face, the dullness in his usually alert eyes, rang a warning, clanging against her temple. "No," he said, walking into the cabin when she waved him in. "She's fine. Just a mild concussion."

"You didn't have to come all the way out here to tell me that, Eric," she said, peering outside before closing the door to the cold wind blowing through her tunic top.

"I know," he said, pacing, running his fingers over his shaved scalp. "It's just... they want me to direct the first two live shows, so she can rest and I, I... I'm not ready. I can't. What if I fuck it up?"

Her usually unflappable assistant verged on

hysterical, his voice pitching high. She stifled a small laugh, knowing he needed someone to talk him off the precipice and went to stand in front of him. "First of all, just breathe before you pass out on me," she said, squeezing his shoulders to brace him while holding his gaze.

He inhaled, blew out the air. Some color returned to his high cheekbones. "Okay… okay. I can do this, right?"

"Of course you can," she said reassuring him. "You know my routine and the way I work in the kitchen. I trust you to get this right."

"Sure, you're right. I'll have no problem with you. You're easy to work for and with," he said, then his hazel eyes clouded, and he pinched the bridge of his nose. "But what about Owen? I've never worked with him before. What if he gives me a hard time? He's charming but, I'm afraid it's all surface level because he gives off vibes like he's hard to please. How will I handle him if he goes off the rails?"

"He's a professional." Albeit a bit temperamental, but he'd never been a jerk while they'd competed for the top slot. "Don't worry about him. We talked this afternoon, coordinated our recipes and finalized our preparations for the shows. He's here to celebrate the grand opening of another flagship restaurant in New York. This will be fun. Try not to worry."

She hugged her assistant. "I'm sorry Angela's out of commission, but I'm thrilled for you. Who knows?

You might get your own show to direct because of this."

"You think so?"

"Take it from me, Eric, anything is possible in this world if we're willing to take risks." She meant the words. Tonight she'd act on her own advice too.

With Brent.

Another chime rang. Eric finally focused on her, the aromas scenting the cabin. "Whoa. I'm interrupting something."

"Not yet," she said, heading toward the door.

"Ha. I understand," he said, following her. "Just be sure to get plenty of rest tonight. If you can."

She laughed. "I will," she said, then opened the door.??

Brent stood on the deck holding a bottle of red wine she recognized from the vineyard near her hometown. "Saxon Cabernet, special selection," he said, stepping inside only to stop when he spotted Eric. "Saw your car. Guess this isn't a dinner for two after all. My mistake."

"No. No mistake." She tilted her head toward Eric. "We just wrapped up an impromptu business meeting."

"Yes. I was just leaving," Eric said as he jammed his hands in his parka's pockets. "See you tomorrow and remember. I need you rested and on top of your game."

"You've got it." Reagan walked him to the door, let

him out. "And be sure to do the same. I know you'll be great."

"Thanks," he said, then loped down the stairs to his replacement rental.

"Whew. Glad I talked him off the proverbial ledge." She turned to Brent. "He's taking over for Angela until she's cleared to work again."

"Good thing he didn't get hurt in that accident. How is she?" he asked, handing her the bottle, then taking off his coat which revealed his gun and holster.

"You always carry?" she asked.

"Comes with the job," he said as he removed his weapon and holster, then hung them under his leather jacket. "Does it bother you?"

"No. My brother was in the DEA, but I'm glad you're not wearing it now. Besides, your quick instincts during the accident stopped things from getting a lot worse than a few bumps and scrapes and smashed cars." She returned to the kitchen and set the bottle down on the counter. "Who'd have thought my jokingly asking you to be my bodyguard on the slopes would become the real thing?"

"Yeah." He wrapped his arms around her from behind. "Good thing. Especially when I happen to like having you in one piece, so I can do things like this." He caressed her waist, stroked down her hips and then cruised his hands up again. "And like this…" Brent edged her around to face him, then anchored her neck and lowered his mouth until it hovered a mere inch from hers.

She inhaled his breath, tasted the kiss before he closed the scant distance lock their mouths together. She coiled her hands around his neck and held on, rocked into him, yielding to the sensations spiraling through her.

REAGAN BROUGHT her body flush to Brent's, pressing herself against him. Her tight nipples poked into his chest, and a soft moan escaped her, the sexy sound arrowing through him straight to his cock.

He hardened, and his pulse thundered in his ears. Heat, the scent of her, raised his temperature to a feverish high. God. He wanted her. Bad.

Their first kiss had been brief, tender. Sweet. This? Hell, there was nothing sweet about how Reagan's lush lips teased his, opening him wider, sliding her tongue inside, exploring.

He fisted his hands in her hair, holding her steady, hungering for more. More of her succulent flavor and her sultry moans. He inhaled them all, drank them in. Greedy, starved. Unable to get enough.

Beeping, insistent and strong, broke through his sex-buzzed brain. He cut off the kiss, still holding her, and gazed into her gleaming dark blue eyes.

She released his neck, pointed to the microwave over the stove beside her. "Dinner calls."

"We could just skip dinner, go straight for dessert."

Reagan nibbled her lower lip. "Tempting." She pressed her hand against his chest. "But I'm not wasting USDA prime beef. Open the wine, pour some while I sear the steaks."

He covered her hand with his, reminded himself she deserved the slow build, but damn. Everything in him wanted to cruise into fast lane, especially his still hard cock. Inhaling a deep breath, he willed a bucket of mental ice down his pants.

Didn't work. The sooner he got away from the only thing he wanted to eat, her, the better.

Brent squeezed her hand, then let her go. "You've got it," he said, moving around her.

"Great. Won't take me long to get everything ready." She shifted around him to open the fridge door.

He rifled through the drawer for the corkscrew, opened the wine and poured two glasses. After placing hers on the counter next to the stove, he carried his to the living area and set it on the fireplace's mantle. Sizzling sounds permeated the air while he stacked kindling, cut logs and lit them with one of the long, wooden matches next to the open hearth.

The flames flickered to life and he drank his wine,

watching her in the kitchen. She'd tied an apron around her waist, which accentuated the flare of her full hips. Her back turned to him, she moved with grace and efficiency while tossing salad, flipping the steaks.

His mouth watered. More for the woman cooking him a meal than for the food itself.

Later, after they'd eaten the delicious food she'd prepared, he helped her carry the empty plates to the sink, started scraping them.

The logs he'd stacked earlier crackled, the orange and yellow flames flickered, warming the room and scenting the air with wood smoke. "Thanks for dinner," he said. "Everything was amazing." The steak had been a perfect medium rare all the way throughout, the potatoes crisp and savory. He'd even enjoyed the salad with the tangy dressing.

But none of that could compare to the delicious person who'd served up the generous plates of food.

"Glad you liked it," she said. "Here, let me help." She reached for the last plate in the sink at the same time he did.

Heat sparked beneath his skin when she accidentally touched his hand. "I've got this." He drew the dish away and loaded it into the small dishwasher. "Besides, you cooked. I clean."

Her gaze locked onto his. The same heat firing along his nerves reflected in her cobalt rimmed eyes. "I like the way you think."

"Excellent." He slid his arms around her waist, pulled her close. He revolved her into the living room and to the sofa in front of fireplace. "Can you guess what I'm thinking right now?"

Her lips parted ever so slightly as her breath hitched. The pulse in the base of her neck fluttered rapidly, matching the drumming in his.

"I'm betting I can," she said, her voice husky. "Dessert?"

Still holding with her with one arm, he traced his index finger down the side of her face, over her rosy cheek and across her lips one by one, then lower still to the hollow in her neck. "You'd be betting right."

She arched her back, bringing her breasts higher, the cleavage within inches of his roving hand. "Then that makes two of us." Reagan bridged the scant distance between them. "And I'm not talking about s'mores."

Brent circled the sensitive spot he'd lasered in on, then drawing a line between her gorgeous, full breasts. "Neither am I."

BRENT'S WHISKEY colored eyes turned dark, the flecks of amber in them sparking more heat than the fire flickering in the hearth. Every cell in her body seemed to come alive, truly alive for the first time in years.

Reagan craved him with an intensity she'd forgotten she possessed. Yet, he waited. And, for an excruciating millisecond that seemed to last forever, she remained paralyzed, unable to act.

But the electricity, the tension spiraling between them unraveled the last remnant of her resistance. She bridged the remaining distance between them to fuse her mouth to his. And then there was the rush, the craving, the wanting racing through her veins and skimming along her nerves, as she took everything he had to offer.

She swept her tongue along the seam of his lips, parting them and gliding it along his. Tasting the wine, the man. She slaked in and out of him, need and demand propelling her.

He cruised his hands down her back, cupped her ass and hitched her closer, his powerful thighs bracing her legs. The ridge of his erection pressed against her. Her panties grew wet and her clit pulsated, throbbed.

Demanding more, she moaned into his mouth, arched her back and raised her breasts into his chest, frenzied, eager for his touch. He cupped both, stroked his thumbs over the puckered peaks. She moaned, skimmed her hands to his waist to jerk his shirt out of the jeans and slide them up his naked, muscular torso.

"This has to go," he said, wrenching his mouth from hers to drag her tunic top over her head. "And this." The bra landed somewhere south on the floor as he released her breasts.

More need flowed, making her wetter. Her scent filled the air, mingled with his clean, masculine aroma.

His irises gleamed hot as he traced his fingers over her exposed breasts, circling closer to her nipples. She inhaled a sharp breath, raising them while caressing his torso, running her hands an inner feminine thrill thrummed along her nerves.

He dropped his gaze to her lips, then back up. Renewed heat flashed, pulsed and flared between them.

God. She couldn't remember the last time a man had looked at her that way. She popped the buttons on his shirt, pushed it off his shoulders, and over his arms.

They stood body-to-body, skin-to-skin and the sensation dizzied her, making her knees buckle.

But he didn't let her fall, anchoring her with one strong arm while cupping one of her breasts, tweaking her sensitized nipple. She fisted her hands in his hair as lust arrowed through her, sent tremors into every erogenous zone.

Reagan ached for him, longing for more. "Brent, I want..."

"Me too." He caught her mouth again, sucking her lower lip into his, then releasing it with a pop. "So goddamn much."

The ridge of his hard cock pressed against her, proving his point. "Then what are we waiting for?" She reached for his waistband, tugged at the belt buckle to loosen it.

"Hold on," he said, stilling her hand.

"I plan on holding you if you'll let me."

He gave her a lopsided smile. "Boots first."

A giggle escaped. "Right." She pushed his chest until he sat on the sofa behind him, then kneeled to take them off. "There. Pants. Now." Reagan glanced at the man dwarfing the couch as she stood to wiggle out of her leggings and oh-so boring panties.

He joined her, moving so fast, her vision blurred momentarily. Before she could refocus, Brent wrapped his arms around her waist to draw her close, the hair on his muscular chest teasing the tips of her nipples.

She circled his neck, and he lowered her to the plush cushions, his full, generous mouth locked onto hers while those hands... oh those hands... they were on her, exploring her like a man possessed.

Hungry for every touch, every caress, she spread her legs, need pooling between them to give him easier access. Tongues tangling, fighting, sliding together, she devoured him over and over.

Brent kneaded her breasts, playing with her nipples one by one, dizzying her, driving her higher. The tension coiling low tightened, tugged, pumped hard.

She hitched her hips, moaned into his mouth. His cock jumped against her leg. So close. So so close. Reagan slipped her hand down, clasped the length, stroked the velvety flesh over granite.

He pumped into her palm while cruising his hand to the apex between her thighs, moving his long fingers over her folds, probing them to drive one into her.

She gasped. Spread wider for him to meet the driving force, wanting to take him deeper, deeper still.

He swept her juices out and over her pulsating clit, circling the bundle of nerves. Stars burst behind her eyes and she cried his name, the sensations powering through her, intense need fired into her nerves, bringing her higher.

Reagan struggled to hang on, lost her grip on her control as her orgasm built. She wrenched her mouth from his. "Brent. I can't... it's too, too-"

"You can. Come for me, Reagan."

He took her mouth again, sucked in her cries, swallowed them as they ripped from her throat. And never let up, increased his pressure, the intensity of his fingers plunging in and out of her making her head spin.

And when he circled her clit faster, stronger, in tandem along with his relentless driving fingers, her orgasm surged through her.

She held onto him, her cries echoing in her ears. "Don't let go, please don't let me go."

"I'VE GOT YOU," Brent promised, his dick growing harder as she flowed around him, her orgasm a rush of liquid and spasms.

He heard more than the need in Reagan's words. He heard the wanting. The yearning. Christ. He couldn't release her and yet...

She slid her hand down his back, over his ass and raised her hips. "Brent, that was, you were... but I hope that's not all you've got planned for dessert."

"Hell no." He shoved the next thought of his head as his cock throbbed, lengthening with all his blood rushing low. "Just give me a second." Somehow, in all the frenzy of stripping, he'd remembered to place his protection on the side table next to the couch.

"Thank God."

Brent laughed. "I figured I'd gamble on a yes tonight." He reached for the foil packet and within moments sheathed himself.

She hitched her hips higher to give him easier access to her sweet, hot pussy. The pungent scent of her arousal mingled with wood smoke, teasing him, dizzying him.

Holding her gaze, the cobalt blue irises both sensual and so goddamn trusting. A band tightened around his chest, making it hard to take in air, to breathe. He wanted to deserve what reflected in those gorgeous, sexy eyes.

"Brent," she whispered, her fingers ghosting over his brow, cheek, mouth.

"I got you," he said again, then took her lips once more and guided his cock between her slick folds.

She opened for him, once more cupping his ass, insistent, demanding more.

He drove into her in one smooth stroke, her pussy walls clenching around him, bringing him all the way to the hilt. God. Yes. This woman. This was where he belonged.

Tight, sweet, wet. Perfect.

He withdrew, drove in again, plunging deeper, faster. Christ, she met him stroke for stroke, her skin slick, slapping against him.

Over and over, he fucked her. Hard. Gave her what she'd demanded. Branding her. Claiming her though he didn't have the right.

His balls tightened, the full force of his ejaculation building with every stroke.

She gasped in his mouth, arched her neck, raising herself, thrusting her full breasts into his torso, the nipples budded into taut berries. He raced one hand over them, caressed the engorged tips, playing with them.

She bucked beneath him, wrenched her mouth from his. "God. Yes. Don't stop."

His cock fucking filled with more blood, got harder than he'd thought possible, and he slammed into her, bringing her to the edge again. "Come with me. Do it," he demanded.

"I will. Holy…"

Her juices flowed over him, hot and creamy. He drove into her one more time, his release shuddering through him until he'd spilled every last drop of himself.

Collapsing, slick with sweat, he took her mouth again, kissing her as if she were an anchor, a lifeline.

# CHAPTER 6

BRENT ROLLED OVER, taking the sheets with him, only to feel a sharp poke in his shoulder. "What?" He rubbed the sleep out of his eyes. "What's wrong?"

"Anyone tell you you're a bed hog?" Reagan asked from the edge of the mattress as she scooted toward him and stole back her share of the covers. "Though I suppose I can forgive you considering how well you used it last night."

"Sorry." He brought her into his arms, snuggling her. "What time is it?" Shadows, dark corners and only one dim light illuminated the room.

"Time for me to get cracking," she said. "Makeup and hair people will have to get a bonus for making me look like I actually got some rest last night. Not that I'm complaining."

He checked his cell phone. Not even seven in the morning. "You start this early?"

"I'm usually up by now, sometimes earlier," she said. "Restaurant hours never stop, not even when I'm officially off the clock."

"Ah, point made." He stroked her arm, trailing his fingers down her silky skin. Skin he'd tasted and touched and explored in multiple ways. And he'd grown addicted to the feel of her, of them together. "Tell you what. How about I make you breakfast while you get ready?"

"You any good in the kitchen?" she asked dubiously.

"I make a mean omelet and coffee's coffee."

"Then you've got a deal." She kissed his cheek and scrambled out of bed. She paused at the bathroom door and shot him a sultry look. "I promise not to use up all the hot water."

"We could shower together."

"So not going to happen. It'll already take a miracle to get me ready for the show."

"I think you look perfect right now."

"That's just because you're a sex addict."

"Go. Take your shower before I prove you right."

As she walked inside, her movements slow and languid, a wave of nostalgia washed through him. How easily they'd slipped into a normal, couple-like routine. Something he hadn't realized he'd missed until he'd accepted this assignment. Just the simplicity of being with someone, enjoying everyday life.

And then the truth he'd denied, shoved into the back of his brain because he'd just wanted her so goddamn much slammed into his gut. If she ever discovered why he'd shown up at Eagle Point, he figured she might not forgive him for concealing the truth. But so far, her brother's over-protectiveness had been misplaced. And she'd never hired him, so technically, he could be off the hook.

*Yeah. Keep telling yourself that big guy. You should have come clean before you had sex with her, but you didn't want to lose out on the chance on really getting to know her... fuck.*

His ass was toast if she learned the original reason for his so-called vacation in Montana.

Naked, he crawled out of bed, made his way to the living room to retrieve his clothes, drew on the bottoms and shirt, leaving it unbuttoned. Then he checked his Glock and magazine of bullets which he'd stashed in his jacket's inner pocket. His cell phone now tucked in his pant pocket, he made his way back to the luxury cabin's small, modern kitchen.

Within minutes, he'd started the coffee and whipped eggs into a frothy mixture while butter melted in the frying pan. Popping whole grain bread into the toaster, he mentally rehashed the events that had led him to this moment.

He liked Reagan. He wanted her. He acted on the heat, the craving.

A heavy feeling dropped into his gut like a rock. Fuck. He'd broken every personal code he had for keeping his hands off his agency's clients with a dumbass rationalization to justify acting on his desire. Not only that, but as far as she was concerned, she'd had sex with a businessman from San Francisco. Doubtful she'd like his actual profession, one that put him in harm's way on a regular basis.

Not after she'd lost the love of her life to a horrific car accident.

But, he reasoned with himself, she'd never have to know how he earned a living. They'd made no promises. This was a holiday fling. Period.

The rock weighing down his stomach splintered into pieces, pummeled him from the inside like gun shot. Yeah. He wasn't just omitting the truth from her. He was deluding himself. He'd slept with her because he wanted way more than a fling, but now he couldn't figure out how to move forward with the reality of his situation wedging a barrier between them.

He poured the egg mix into the pan, then hunted for cheese in the fridge. Sure enough, she had plenty.

"Smells delicious," Reagan said, sliding her arms around his waist and resting her head on the space between his shoulders. "Thanks for making me breakfast."

She smelled fresh, clean with a hint of the vanilla that seemed to follow her everywhere. "Only fair," he said easily, though his heart drummed faster, a tympani of want warring with guilt.

"Still, a girl could get used to having a sexy man in her kitchen on a regular basis."

His back muscles tightened, pain lanced up his spine with the speed of a lightning bolt. Whatever they'd said to each other about temporary flings or holiday romances had morphed into something different in so many ways. He didn't know how he could take that change and run with it later. Plus, her history reared in his brain. How could he ask her to take a risk on him given his real career?

"I'll get the plates and cutlery," she said, releasing him and moving to the cupboard.

She sounded as stiff as his back and neck muscles. He ignored the instant urge to turn around and hug her, reassure her. Better to have her think he was an asshole. Right? No. He didn't want to hurt her because... fuck... he was so royally hosed.

He folded omelet, sliced in two with the spatula. "You've got a full schedule this week." Brent placed the omelet halves onto both plates, grabbed the toast and plopped them on.

The silence in the room hung between them like a heavy curtain, blocking them from really seeing each other. Fine. He'd go back to his cabin, keep up appearances, pull away before he did permanent harm to her, and him too.

His cell phone buzzed in his pocket, he dug it out,

read the text. A stinging sensation prickled into his fingertips and arced into his temples. The fucking accident might not have been a simple skid over ice. The examiner had to run further analysis. And until those suspicions were confirmed, Brent's assignment officially went from doing a favor for an overprotective brother to making sure his sexy, currently pissed-off client, didn't get into the line of fire.

"Any chance we'll get to see each other today?" Not that he'd let her out of his sight, but he'd planned to watch over her from a discreet distance. No way he wanted to tip her off now.

She carried the plates to the small table. "Sure," Reagan said, avoiding his gaze. "That'd be nice, but don't feel like you have to see me out of some duty. You're on vacation."

Fuck, he'd blown this entire situation to hell and back again. "Thought you'd be part of that now." He brought the coffee he'd poured and set a cup in front of where she now sat. "We had fun. And neither of us are in it for the long haul, but why not keep having fun?" He lifted his eyebrows, tilted his head toward her while flashing his best one hundred watt smile.

She sliced into her omelet carefully. Way too carefully. Yep. Definitely upset.

"You know, Brent, I didn't mean anything by what I said earlier. But you sure had a strong reaction," she said, now holding his gaze with hers. "While I'm not interested in long term anythings, I don't like feeling like I'm just an easy lay. So maybe you should take your offer somewhere else."

~

REAGAN BIT INTO THE OMELET, the flavor like sawdust to her, waited for Brent to reply while she chewed slowly. He'd gone from flirty, easy and relaxed this morning to freaking stiff as a plank. Hell, he'd acted like she'd asked him to walk an actual plank after what she'd said earlier.

Where had the guy she'd had wild sex with all night long gone?

His whiskey eyes didn't shift, refusing to budge from hers, unwavering. But the subtle shift of his knife in his hand and the muscle jumping in his strong jaw revealed a different story.

She recognized the tension all too well. After all, she had a brother and his friends, including Scott, had certain tells whenever they tried to skirt around the truth or cover something up.

His Adams apple bobbed up and down as Brent lowered his knife to the plate and leaned back, the movement rocking his chair ever so slightly. "You're right," he said after another tense beat of silence. "You deserve better from me."

A flush of adrenaline tingled through her body, heating her cheeks. She'd expected him to disagree with her, deny her reaction. Maybe even mansplain his way out of her accusation. She should be relieved, her secret still safely buried, but somehow she wanted him to be that man and his words stung. She hid her confusion, the emotional tumult rolling through her with a calm façade she didn't feel. "True. I do." Reagan cut her omelet again, still holding his whiskey-colored eyes with hers. "So why'd you act like I'd sentenced you to a lifetime with a ball and chain earlier?"

"I got my signals crossed and took what you said way too seriously." Brent reached over, covered her free hand with his. "Could you cut me a break and give me a chance to make it up to you?"

An electrical charge sparked into her skin, traveled into all her naughty lady bits. She shivered despite the room's warmth. One touch and he'd managed to get past her guard. "I enjoyed our date and last night was great," she said, jerking her hand free, then pushing away from the table. She couldn't let him see or know her instant reaction.

"But?"

Reagan stood and picked up her dish, clinking the cutlery onto the plate. "But I need to focus on my job right now." She squared her shoulders and pivoted on her heel, then made her way back to the small kitchen. "Don't bother helping with the cleanup. Just let yourself out." She needed him to leave before she did something stupid like cry in front of him. She didn't want a long term commitment, but she'd liked him. And he'd acted like he felt the same way.

She scraped the uneaten omelet into the trashcan, dumped her plate into the sink and turned around to see Brent standing too.

"I really am sorry." He buttoned his shirt while he spoke. "More than you can possibly know."

Why did he sound so, so... sad? And why did his plain spoken words sound true like he really cared more than he wanted to admit? She shook off the thoughts, not wanting to go there mentally. "So am I," she said resolutely, desperate to hide the whirlwind of confusing emotions pummeling behind her sternum. "I hope the rest of your vacation is *fun*."

He rubbed the space between his brows, shook his head. "Doubtful now," he said before he made his way to the entryway and grabbed his coat. "Be sure to lock up after I leave."

The door closed behind him with a soft snick.

She slumped against the counter, the pushed away and followed his advice to slide the deadbolt in place. Then, after loading her dishwasher, she shoved on her winter gear and geared herself up for what she'd come to Eagle Point Ranch to do.

Losing herself in working, filming the show, would effectively wash the ever sexy Brent Lancaster out of her system permanently. At least, she hoped it would, she thought as she drove back to the luxury ranch's main building.

Rounding the final corner to enter the parking lot, she hit a bump and the SUV skidded. She tasted acid, panic raced through her scalp, raising the hairs on her head. Tamping down the fear, she turned into the skid and regained control immediately.

Still, her heartbeat thundered in her ears until she safely parked and exited her vehicle. Clutching her crossbody bag's straps, she hurried up the stairs that led to the entrance and stepped onto the grand wrap-around porch. Moving to open the door, a large hand beat her to the handle.

"After you," Brent said, stepping beside her to let her in.

Her pulse accelerated, thundered in her ears. The restaurant didn't start serving for another hour. "You following me?" she asked.

"No. I'm supposed to be here," he said. "Meeting with the general manager about providing security here. Looks like the Brotherhood Protectors are plenty busy these days and Hank asked me to touch base with her."

"I thought you were here on vacation," she said as she walked inside.

"I am," he said easily. "But when she heard I was coming here, she contacted me about hiring my company."

Reagan had met the general manager during their tour and had liked the woman on the spot. The single mother had a great sense of humor, was insightful and smart too. And, given all those positive check marks in her favor, her gorgeousness along with her size perfect body, would attract any red-blooded man.

Jealousy, unwelcome as hell, wove through her. "Well, I guess you're not going to have any trouble having a good time while you're here after all," she said, feigning a breezy attitude she absolutely didn't feel.

Disappointment tripped along her spine, but Reagan clamped down the ridiculous emotion, walking away from Brent before she exposed herself to his way too scrutinizing gaze.

# CHAPTER 7

B RENT WAITED for her to greet her makeup and hair stylists before moving to the chairs in front of the large fireplace. Oversized logs crackled and fired sparks up into the chimney. Checking in with his commander with the recent developments, he forwarded the information to his agency's headquarters in California via his encrypted cell phone.

**How is Reagan doing? She suspect anything?**

He paused, hesitated in answering. The truth? Too personal. And his rationalization for sleeping with her, wanting to be with her in more than a physical sense, dipped into the guilt zone as he read his commander's text. After leaving Reagan's cabin, Brent had returned to his to watch over her via his surveillance cameras. **She has no idea about the possible danger. I'd like to keep it that way.** Brent replied.

Other than seeing the sadness in her face, nothing out of the ordinary happened. The sadness brought an ache to his chest that refused to evaporate.

**Her brother will want to step up security if this intel pans out. He'll do anything to protect her.**

So far Brent had been the only person who'd hurt Reagan. She might have every reason not to spend time with him, but now he had to make sure he never let her out of his sight. Later, he'd wrap his brain around what to do about the feelings she'd stirred in him.

**I'm in constant contact with Hank Patterson. We'll mobilize if necessary.**

**Excellent.**

He signed off, made his way to the concierge's desk, poured a cup of fresh coffee. Drinking it, he crossed the floor to the floor-to-ceiling windows overlooking the ranch's vast property. Snow covered the grounds and the staff outside prepped a pair of sleighs with holiday garland. Inside, he heard the clatter of the restaurant crew gearing up for the morning breakfast rush. Cutlery clinked against china, orders called by the managers to the servers, and the scents of cinnamon and sugar filled the air.

"Hey," Eric's voice cut into his thoughts. "Didn't expect to see you here this early. Where's Reagan?"

Brent turned to face her assistant and now director. He'd gotten a great opportunity after the accident, but Reagan hadn't been in charge of the decision to put Eric in the director's seat. "Already on the set," he said. "Getting ready."

"Great. You drive her?" the man asked, knowing just exactly where Brent had been the night before.

"No." He'd run a background check on the entire cast and crew prior to arriving in Eagle Point. Nothing stood out. He glanced at his agency issued spyware watch, the recording ability set to on. "Got a meeting with the general manager in fifteen." But he'd also seen her skidding on her way to the ranch's main building. He'd check out her SUV after he ditched Eric.

"Ah. You want to watch today's filming? We've got a studio audience set up. Would love to see you there."

"What time?" he asked nonchalantly though he jumped at the idea of being closer to her without tipping her off per his orders. But he had to fake his meeting first or he'd raise suspicion.

"Not for another hour and a half." Eric waved. "Owen. You ready for the big day?"

The chef from New York sauntered toward them. "Absolutely. Just went over the menu with the ranch's staff and we're good to go. Hey," he said. "You the hero of the day that saved Reagan from this dope's slip and slide?"

Hero? More like an asshole. "I just pulled her out of the SUV's path. No big deal."

"Is to me," Owen said, stretching out his hand.

"And to the entire crew. Reagan's the heart of *Cooking Thyme*. Without her, they'd have to reboot the entire show and go in another direction."

After giving the man a firm grip, Brent smiled without meaning it. Owen Davidson was the face of the Davidson fleet of five star restaurants located in and around New York City, but Brent didn't buy the guy's schtick. He'd never trusted guys who oozed metro charm and compliments. But being a playboy didn't make the chef his chief suspect.

Yet.

"I'll pop by later, check the show out if my meeting doesn't run too late," he said to Eric. "See you around."

He left the two men, strolling toward the hallway that led to the ranch's offices, then veered over to the main entrance and stepped outside.

The day before he'd nabbed her fob's code. Now he went to her rental, brought out the device to transmit the same radio frequency to jam the signal that locked the car. After opening the driver side door, he popped the front hood to check the battery connections. Nothing. Brake fluid and oil levels came next. All at required levels. Closing the hood and kneeling to examine the undercarriage, he mulled over how to take Eric up on his offer.

Tires solid. But.. Fucking brake line had a slight cut-precise and deliberate. He clenched his jaw, narrowed his eyes, anger flashing through him. One wrong turn or ice on the road or hitting a bump could snap the motherfucker in two. He withdrew his cell phone, snapped a picture of the damaged line.

Was this coincidence or planned? He'd follow up with the rental company. And he definitely had an in with Reagan after securing one with Eric.

Before he could tuck his cell phone back in his pocket, a text flashed on the screen. He read the message. Sheriff's suspicions had been confirmed. The report gave him the answer he needed.

Standing, he wracked his brain for a way to get past her guard again. One thing he knew for sure, she might not like him much as a person, but she still wanted him. He'd seen the flash of envy in her blue eyes before she'd shuttered them and hustled off to meet her show's crew.

He made his way back to the ranch's front entrance as the pain behind his sternum intensified, lanced deeper. He rubbed the spot with the heel of his hand before opening the doors. He hated that he gave her the wrong idea about him. He'd lied to himself when he'd told himself they'd both be better off as long as he continued to do so.

Now he'd have to ramp up the charm himself.

Killed him a little inside that he'd acted like the jerk of the year this morning, but ultimately he'd believed he didn't have a choice. He certainly shouldn't have had sex with her. Period.

But now that he'd gotten a taste of her, could he

keep his hands to himself while still trying to reach beyond her defenses, so he could protect her? So he could one day make his subterfuge up to her at the right time?

Walking through the ranch's foyer toward the restaurant's hostess stand, he knew nothing could stop him from eating breakfast in the same restaurant where she filmed her show. The sheriff's text along with the sheered brake line had given him extra motivation to step up his game.

He'd do everything in his power to keep her sexy ass alive even if it meant admitting the truth.

"So how did last night with Mr. Tall Hot and Sexy Stetson go?" Eric asked.

Reagan closed her eyes as her makeup artist applied shadow. "It went... I don't want to talk about it."

"He's here."

"I know." She didn't like Brent's presence in the same building one bit. But he had a right to go wherever he pleased as long as he avoided her. "Not that I care."

"Sure," her stylist said. "Then explain the puffy eyes and shadows I just had to cover up."

A shiver crawled into the back of her neck, making the bones brittle as ice. She'd spent the better

part of her morning ritual swallowing disappointment and tears, but her crew didn't need to know
every detail of her personal life. "Nothing happened
with him. I just didn't sleep well," she said, now
staring at her flawless reflection in the mirror across
from her. "We ate, talked about the best ways to
produce and market my secret special marinating
and basting sauces."

Not the truth. She'd shared her plans with a few
people on the show's staff along with her former
rival Owen who'd offered to showcase her products
in his restaurants.

Her stylist applied another stroke of blush on her
cheeks. "Tell that to someone who'll believe it. I saw
the way you were looking at him yesterday."

"When did you... oh never mind. How'd I look at
him?" Was she really that obvious? Inwardly, she
rolled her eyes and shook her head. God, sometimes
she wished her emotions didn't come across like an
open book, but she'd gotten the current gig with her
genuine personality.

"Well?" she asked again.

"Like he was a big juicy steak and you couldn't
wait to take a bite and eat the whole damn thing."

She inhaled a breath, counted to ten, then
released the air slowly, trying to make the embarrass-
ment flushing through her evaporate. "Honestly, we
just talked business. No big deal," she said, scrutinizing the final touches the makeup artist had added

to her glam. "But thanks for making me look better than I could possibly do on my own." Reagan meant every word. Her stylist was a true genius at beautifying her.

"You've got an easy face to style"

"Ha. I'm glad you think so." She'd never been a total girly girl. Not when she'd been hanging out with her brother and his friends, cooking in her parents' family restaurant, or serving up dogs and burgers at the snack stand during high school football season.

That Scott Harlow had even noticed her had been a minor miracle. But she'd taken a serious effort to make her high school crush look at her like more than his best friend's pesky younger sister.

"I told you to get some rest last night," Eric said, bringing her back to reality.

She glanced at her bare ring finger, then back at her reflection. A lot had changed since she'd gotten that first kiss during a bonfire held at their favorite river cove hangout.

Shifting her glance from the mirror to her PA and temporary director, she shot him a warning glance. If only Eric hadn't been freaking out at her cabin when Brent had shown up for dinner. "I got a case of the nerves," she said in a matter-of-fact tone that also stated he keep the details of her date under wraps.

Eric nodded slightly. "You've been hosting the show for a year," he said. "You'll be fine."

She relaxed back in her chair. Thank god he'd gotten her message. "Live filming, no way to edit out mistakes or bloopers," she said. "That all adds up to one jittery show host."

"Relax. I can handle your nerves until Angela is back behind the camera on Wednesday," he said. "Meanwhile, let's get rolling. We film in half an hour." Eric pushed away from the wall where he'd been leaning. "I'm heading out to prep the audience and touch base with Owen."

"Great. I'm looking forward to meeting them. They'll take the edge off," she said.

"Maybe, maybe not."

A bunch of jellybeans bounced in her tummy. Besides the skeletal early morning ranch staff, one person sprang to mind. One tall, hot and wearing a Stetson to be accurate. *Please tell me you didn't...* "What do you mean" she asked, pressing her hand to her stomach to will the real nerves to get under control.

"I wish I hadn't asked this one particular guy to join us on the set." He moved around Reagan. "But I thought he'd be a welcome addition when I did."

"Aha. Not a big deal? Doubtful." Her stylist stopped packing up her brushes and palettes of color. "I can't wait to see how this plays out."

"Please tell me he said thanks, but no."

"No can do," Eric said. "Sorry, but I didn't think including him would be a problem."

"I'm a professional." Reagan squared her shoulders, stood and raised her chin. "No way will I let him distract me from I have to do on the set if he decides to be part of the live audience." She breezed away from the makeup mirror with what she hoped gave the appearance of total calm, total control.

But on the inside, the jumping jellybeans in her tummy bounced like crazy, zipped into her nerves and pinged into her veins. She trembled, half afraid Brent would be waiting for her front and center on the set.

Half afraid he wouldn't be there which would, for some ridiculous female pride reason, disappoint and hurt her even more.

## CHAPTER 8

"WHY ARE YOU HERE?" Reagan asked, crossing her arms.

"To support your show," Brent said. "And to grovel again." He held up his first gambit, a poinsettia plant potted in silver and gold foil with a huge Christmas tartan bow around the brim.

She narrowed her eyes, but, to his relief, reached for the plant. "It's beautiful, but you didn't have to go to the trouble."

"I did," he said, peering over her shoulders to the set beyond. "I wanted to see you again and if this is the only way I can, I will."

"You hardly seem like the type who cares about pulling together a holiday dinner with all the trimmings."

"Point made, but I am the type who cares about the person prepping the meal."

"You care?"

"Yes. I do. I screwed up, but I won't do it again." He mentally crossed his fingers while holding her gaze, inhaling her delicious scent of vanilla and her unique essence. "I promise. Please. Give me another chance to prove I'm not a first class jerk." Though she'd boot him right back into the asshat territory if she discovered his original reason for bumping into her. Though everything that had happened afterward had been based on real attraction, desire. The deep yearning to explore the emotions she'd sparked in him.

She pursed her lush lips, stroked one of the pink petals. "You willing to forgo the extracurricular nighttime activity to be with me?"

His breath bottled in his chest when he realized her ring finger still remained bare. Lucky for her he'd already vowed to keep his paws to himself in the going all the way department. "I just want to spend time with you. If that means just going out on dates and hanging together, that's cool with me." Because she needed his protection until he figured out who'd cut the brake line and set up the accident the other day. And he needed time to figure out how to keep her as a part of his life after this mission.

Everyone, including Eric, was on his suspect list despite his earlier background checks.

Reagan inhaled a breath, her full breasts rising and falling, tempting him, making him itchy to touch and explore them again. He shoveled internal dirt over the instant attraction buzzing through him, waited for her reply.

"I'll think about it." She tilted her head toward the area the show's crew had cordoned off in the restaurant. "Grab a seat. *Cooking Thyme* starts filming in fifteen minutes."

She turned away, walked toward the set without glancing back. He followed her and sat through the show, unable to keep his eyes off her lush ass. Damn. She had a fine butt and he'd just promised himself, and her, he'd never touch it again. At least, not until he'd completed this operation.

This assignment had all kinds of pitfalls, dangers included more than stopping a potential killer. They included his cock suffering from sex deprivation. He'd have to take a lot of cold showers, maybe even spend extra time on the nearby slopes to keep his shit under control.

He sat through the show, tasted the dish samples Reagan and her temporary co-host, Owen, created. And wanted a taste for a whole lot more than the succulent bourbon-maple glazed spiral cut ham and side dishes.

But no. He'd reminded himself to limit his tastes to the food she offered throughout the week, not her.

Easy. No.

Especially now as they walked out of Al's Diner into the cold air, the frigid wind slapping his face.

Beside him, Reagan shivered. "The temperatures drop to a billion below freezing in Montana at night."

"Come here." He wrapped his arm around her shoulders, warming her. "Won't be long before we're inside my SUV." He'd remotely started the vehicle and the purring engine would have the heater running.

"The burgers and fries are worth freezing my ass off." She quickened her pace as they approached the rental. "And meeting Al is a bonus. Knowing he's all bark, no bite will make filming our show in two days."

"I'll get you there if the rental company hasn't sent a replacement." Though he'd made sure they wouldn't, using his agency's vast network of connections to ensure her safety. From today on, he'd be her driver.

"Yes. Good thing you called the road service before I drove it to my cabin," she said, her lips chattering. "Talk about a lucky break to have you around to check it out. Glad you saw me slip and slide into the parking lot this morning."

"See? You need me." He opened the passenger door, inhaled the interior's leather scent as she stepped inside.

"I could get a ride from Eric or any of the other show crew members."

"True, but I consider this a bonus to getting to know you better."

He closed the door, then rounded the rental to climb into the driver's seat. After the drive back to the luxury ranch, he walked her to the cabin.

"Well," she said, holding his gaze. "I'll see you tomorrow. We've got a show to film live at Sadie Patterson's. Delaney Walker will be there too."

As would their husbands. Additional protection he'd contacted to provide backup on the set.

They'd talked about her childhood, his, during dinner. He'd opened up a bit about his background but didn't reveal the darker corners of his world. Then, and now, he'd survived a lot.

But so had she.

The cabin's exterior walls sheltered them from the bitter blast of arctic wind while soft, plump snowflakes fell all around them, danced on her lashes and cheeks. "I'll pick you up tomorrow at ten." He framed her face with his gloved hands and brushed her lips with his, giving her a chaste kiss. "Good night, Reagan."

"Good night." She used her keycard to let herself inside. "See you in the morning."

Then the light and cozy interior's heat shut him out. He waited several beats, making sure she locked up. Then he went to his SUV, grabbed his infrared goggles out of the gear bag he'd stowed in the back along with extra fire power. Carefully, he circled the cabin, looking for any evidence of possible intruders.

Snow covered any footprints that might have

been left behind and the skeletal tree limbs revealed nothing lurking in the shadows. He checked in with his commander in California who confirmed he'd relay the info to her brother in Italy. And tonight, Brent would continue monitoring her from…

A scream shattered the air, bringing a rush of adrenaline to his extremities. Reagan. His pulse accelerated, and dread oozed into his blood. Bracing his gun, he returned to the stairs that led to her door while glancing around the perimeter.

Nothing but snow, trees swaying in the biting wind, and the sound of a howl in the distance. Tamping down the internal instinct to rush in, he crept up the stairs, his gun loaded and ready to fire if necessary.

Once at the top, he pressed his back flat against the exterior wall, Reagan's shriek piercing the air once more. Carefully, he inserted his agency's pass key into the door's slot, pushed the handle down and dropped low to ease his way inside.

"OH MY GOD." Reagan stared at the clothes littering her bedroom floor along with the scattered files, some of them emptied. Even worse, her side table's drawer had been pulled out, the contents missing. Her rings gone. "Why would anyone take my wedding bands? Why? Why? Why?" She sank to her knees and pounded the floor.

Tears burned behind her eyes and she pressed her palms against them, heat shuddering through her. "I… who…"

Strong arms encircled her. "We'll find out who later," Brent said softly. "Right now, we've got to alert the ranch's security department. Get them here. Don't touch a thing."

"How did you get in here?"

"I own a security company, remember?" he said. "I heard you scream. Not hard for me to break in."

"You heard me? How?" Confusion whirled through her brain. "Weren't you already on your way back to your cabin?" A niggle of suspicion wormed its way into her mind, took root at the base of her skull.

"Thought I'd take a look around the perimeter, make sure nothing unusual was around before I headed to my place."

Her heart thrummed a warning in her ears. Sure. She was glad he'd been around when she discovered the break-in, but his interest in her safety seemed way too convenient. "I didn't hire you to be my security guard, but I guess I should be relieved you acted like one tonight." She hugged herself, still unable to comprehend the mess she'd stumbled on in her bedroom.

Brent covered her arms with his. "I wanted to

make sure you were all right," he said. "The brake line cut looked too clean to be accidental."

"Thanks, but why do I get the feeling you've been shadowing me ever since we met?" She twisted around to gaze into his whiskey-colored eyes. "Who are you really, Brent? Why are you so interested in spending time with me?"

He pursed his lips and a muscle jumped in his jaw as he glanced to the right, then back into her eyes. "I like you. A lot."

His arms suddenly seemed like chains. She pushed out of them and stood on still wobbly legs. "But?" she asked, staring at him as he rose to stand in front of her.

"But your brother called in a favor with my company, asked me to send someone out to keep an eye on you while you filmed your show."

"Why would he even know about your..." she clammed up, the pieces coming together in a whack-a-mole puzzle. "I always knew there was something more to my brother's story about his move to Italy. I never had a problem believing how much he loves my sister-in-law, but I couldn't imagine him raising grapes in Tuscany after he quit the DEA." Something else had lured him besides the woman he loved. Her brother had been chasing adventure his entire life.

Brent had the same aura, the same take-charge and ultra-protective personality.

"I can't tell you everything, but this much is true,"

Brent said, shoved his fingers through his short brown hair. "I was between assignments, my commander asked me to follow up on your brother's request as a precaution. I never meant for things to get out of control between us."

"So having sex with me wasn't part of your description?"

"No. I normally don't fool around with clients, but I... ah... technically your brother hired me and..." He scrubbed his face. "I know I fucked up, but I like you. A lot. But I shouldn't have screwed around with you."

Spots flashed in her vision and her breath bottled in her chest, making it hard to draw in air. She'd been hurt before, lost more than she'd ever anticipated early in her marriage. Brent's confession paled in comparison, but still, his words wounded, stung like she'd been attacked by angry wasps.

"But you had sex with me anyway. Then you pushed me away, acted like a jerk, then you chased after me, asking for another chance." She fisted her hands, then crossed her arms. "Why? What else is going on that you and my brother and everyone else knows but me?"

"The accident that put your show's director out of commission wasn't one. I found out this morning."

"So the only reason you're with me now is to make sure trouble doesn't find me." Her female ego high fived the fact that he'd admitted to wanting her, but he'd hurt her just the same by not telling her everything from the get-go. She didn't know what disappointed her more. His subterfuge or that she'd fallen for his dumb poinsettia and the date at the diner like a first class idiot. "Fine. Clearly, my brother made the right call to have someone come here to watch over me, but I highly doubt he'll like hearing about your methods. I'm surprised you didn't try to move in with me to keep an eye on me 24/7."

"I already had surveillance in place before you arrived."

"You installed cameras? You've been watching me all this time?" She moved around him and out of the bedroom, outrage propelling her. The invasion of her privacy, the complete lack of consideration of her feelings in the matter, floored her. "I know I should be grateful, but right now I'm just so upset I could throat punch someone, including my brother."

She wanted Brent to leave but knew deep down she couldn't reject the protection he offered. She might be hurt and angry, but her pride didn't extend to taking dumb risks with her life.

Now she couldn't shake the man even if she tried. And when she went to open a bottle of wine, he took the corkscrew from her trembling hands. "We didn't think anything would happen," he said, deftly opening it and pouring her a glass. "Figured your brother was being over-protective, but now I'm glad he contacted our branch of the agency."

She drank a healthy swallow, let the ruby red liquid soothe her burning throat and calm the riot stampeding against her ribcage. "I am too."

"Good. Then you understand that I'm not leaving your side until the threat is neutralized," he said.

"Absolutely," Reagan said, her hand steady and her mind settling into a dull pattern of thought. "What if I never found out? What if no one was after me? What would you have told me when your *vacation* ended? When we went our separate ways?" Though she'd been determined to focus on her career, her future, without benefit of a man as a permanent fixture in her life, she'd begun to weave possibilities of a different kind with Brent.

All of those possibilities evaporated tonight. Fair enough. She couldn't give him what he really wanted anyway. One day he'd hang up his holster and settle down, build a family. A life. Just like her brother had done after he'd quit the DEA.

But she damn well wanted him to tell her himself.

# CHAPTER 9

BRENT STALLED, searching for an answer, but he couldn't find one Reagan deserved. One he wished he could give her, but the fire in her blue eyes, the flaring nostrils meant he'd royally blown any chance with her, real or even one forged by an ongoing lie.

"Reagan, I can't be the kind of man you need," he said carefully, remembering her excellent skill in handling razor sharp knives. "Most of what I told you earlier is true, but there are aspects to my job that I'll never be able to share with anyone, not even someone I care about a lot."

"You care?" She drank more wine. "I didn't expect more from you than a nice holiday fling, but you made me believe you wanted me, wanted to get to know me, especially after what happened this morning."

The favor he'd done for his agency, her brother,

turned rotten and his stomach curdled. He'd earned her disappointment in spades when he continued to keep the truth from her. But deep down he'd been searching for a way to salvage some part of this relationship in the future. "I don't know what I'd have done, but I couldn't walk away from you without trying make this, us, work in the future."

"You lied to me from the get-go," she said. "If you had just told me about the threat, the issues surrounding the details about the accident, I'd have accepted the protection without question."

"I realize that now."

"Too bad you didn't come to that conclusion this morning." She set her empty glass on the counter beside the sink. "But even though the damage is done, I won't stop you from doing your job. You still calling the ranch's security people?"

Her blue eyes had grown into cold, chips of ice. A heavy weight pressed down on his shoulders. "I can't trust them. They could be in on this behind the scenes," he said. "I've already contacted Hank Patterson with the Brotherhood Protectors. They're my backup while I'm here."

"Great," she said, moving around him to walk into the living area. "I assume you're contacting him about what happened tonight. Are you able to process the crime scene in my bedroom now or will you wait until tomorrow?"

"I've got equipment at my cabin," he said. "We'll

lock up here, head over there. You're staying with me until we catch the bastard who trashed your bedroom."

Reagan glanced at her bare fingers. "Whoever did this stole my wedding and engagement bands. I want them found and returned to me." She tucked her hands into her jean pockets. "Am I allowed to take anything with me or is everything off limits?"

He scrubbed his hand over his face, then tunneled his fingers through his hair. A heavy feeling pressed down on his shoulders like he'd been carrying a boulder for hours. Maybe if he'd been honest with Reagan, she'd already have been in his cabin, safe and her property, her stuff untouched. But her brother had been adamant about not playing that hand unless absolutely necessary.

The time had arrived. And he never regretted anything more than he did right now.

"Pack a bag with your toiletries, a change of clothes and something to sleep in," he said after a moment of silence that hung between them as if a wall had been erected between them.

"I'll need my paperwork and laptop to prep for the show tomorrow too"

"Bring everything," he said. "I'll run a diagnostic on your files, look for hackers."

"I hope no one stole my recipes."

"Same. But don't worry," he said. "I'll use my video footage to track down who broke into your cabin.

Doubt whoever did left behind prints and yours are all over the place."

"True. I'll get my things," she said, making her way back to the bedroom.

After she returned with a small overnight bag, he guided her to his SUV, surveying the area while shielding her. Five minutes later, they arrived at his cabin. A mirror to hers, but without the homey feel she'd created while staying at the ranch.

"Where's the surveillance equipment?" she asked, holding her bag as she walked in.

"Nowhere obvious." He bolted the doors, tried to ignore the sweet, spicy scent of her filling his nostrils. Failed. He may have screwed up when he screwed her, but he still wanted her. "I'll take a look at what's on the tape while you get some shuteye." Then he stepped away from her to break the connection and crossed the floor to the fireplace's mantle.

"First of all, I want to see who stole my rings. And second, where do you propose I sleep?"

Reagan's voice hitched higher and she clutched her bag tighter and he could see the whites of her knuckles. "You're emotionally drained. Let me handle this while you take my bed." He pointed to the small hallway leading to the room. "I'll hunker down on the pullout sofa after I review the tapes. And you'll see who stole your rings if I catch them in action. I promise."

Her mouth parted, and she covered it with a

trembling hand. "I don't know if I'll be able to rest after what happened tonight," she said, her lips still hidden by her shaking fingers.

"Hold on," he said, returning to her and wrapping his arm around her shoulders. "You're in shock." Brent guided her to the sofa. "Sit."

She didn't argue, dropping to the plush cushions.

He draped a throw blanket over her. "Wait here while I get you some water."

"I couldn't move if I wanted to," she said, the bag she'd carried slipping onto the floor. "Do you mind if I stay here while you check the videos?"

"Do whatever makes you feel better," he said, meaning it.

"What would make me feel better is forgetting this ever happened."

He didn't know if she meant the break-in or having sex with him. "Everything will be okay. I promise." At least, physically, he could protect her. Emotionally? Not so much.

He'd once been on the receiving end of that kind of pain, suffered for his grief after losing his mother to cancer. Now another shard lanced through him for the pain he'd caused Reagan.

He shoved down the regret. No point in going over all his missteps in that department. The only way he'd make up for hurting Reagan was to do what he'd been asked to do. Keep her sexy ass alive. Then he'd get her back to Virginia where her brother's covert agency headquarters could continue their ongoing, undercover protection of her without her ever being the wiser.

His chest ached, and the air bottled briefly in his lungs. He wished he could be more to her even now, especially when he could give his own family what they deserved most: his time and attention and love. Something his stern father failed at epically after his mother passed away.

One of the reasons he'd left the military to join CRUSH had been to create that opportunity. Too bad the opportunity had arrived in the form of a quasi-case where he'd had to hide why he'd bumped into her to begin with the first day he'd met her.

After bringing her a glass of water and two ibuprofen pills, he went back to the mantle, crouched down to reach inside the flute. Within seconds, he'd retrieved his recording equipment. He stood and carried the equipment to a table tucked in the corner of the cabin's kitchen area.

Focusing on retrieving the video footage, he put on his headphones and looked at the first time - stamped video from earlier that evening. Reagan came on screen. At the same time, she sat beside him.

He went still, sucked in a breath and stopped the recording. "Are you sure you don't want to go to bed?" If she didn't vacate the chair, he'd lose control over his tightly held physical desire to hold and comfort her. "If you're too tired to host the show tomorrow, we'll tip off the person behind the vandalism and the tampering."

"I don't want to be alone," she said softly, holding the blanket he'd given her over her shoulders and covering her upper body with the fleece. "I mean, I can't stand the idea of even going into the bedroom when there's someone out there after me. And I have no idea why anyone would want to hurt me."

"Neither do I," he said. "But you've got me." If only he hadn't hidden behind self-denials and rationalizations before. Maybe then she'd trust him. Not just to protect him, but to be there for her no matter what happened.

REAGAN'S INSIDES STILL TREMBLED despite the water, the warmth of Brent's body radiating heat through the blanket she gripped with icy fingers. She inhaled a deep breath, still let down and yet somehow relieved about the reason he'd first stepped into her life, but she meant her words.

She couldn't face the rest of the night without him by her side.

"I'll be right here," he said. "No one can hurt you while you're under my protection. You really do need to get some sleep. The show is filming tomorrow, and we'll need to account for the drive time to White Oak Ranch. It'll be an early start."

"I won't be able to sleep if I go to bed without someone with me," she said, long ago nights and their harsh memories had bubbled to the surface after she discovered her ransacked bedroom. Then she'd suffered from insomnia so intense she thought she'd never get over her losses.

And though Brent hadn't been upfront with her, he'd told her the truth the minute she'd confronted him. Whatever hadn't been true between them, his tenderness and the way he'd held her only one night before had been real. Still, she couldn't let that sway her from keeping her hands to herself from this point forward.

She glanced at his handsome profile. A muscle jumped in his temple and his Adam's Apple bobbed up and down twice. "I've got to check this footage," he said. "You sure you're up to viewing who might have invaded your privacy, stolen your wedding bands and put your life in jeopardy?"

"I'd rather know who's after me than live with uncertainty."

"There's no guarantee we'll be able to identify the culprit."

She shifted closer to his chair, brushed her leg against his. Not to seduce him into saying yes, but to draw more of his strength, power and heat. For now. Later, she'd rely on herself as she'd done before. "We'll know more than we did half an hour ago."

Brent paused, then pressed play and her empty

cabin came into view again. Minutes passed before the first sign of the intruder entered the screen.

"Got him," he said, zooming in on the person dressed in all black. "Crap. Face is covered with mask and goggles."

She sighed. "Then we don't know who did this to me. My things."

"Might not see the person's face, but we can learn a lot by how he moves around the space." He brought the scene into a wide angle. "Confident. Like he knows his way around your space already."

Her stomach quivered, and she cleared her throat before speaking. "Eric's the only one who's been in my cabin and he'd never..." she stopped when the person disappeared from view into the bedroom. "Where's the bedroom footage?"

"Not here."

"You didn't put it under surveillance?" Suddenly the thought of their wild and crazy night of sexy times flashed, bringing a rush of heat into places that had no right to be turned on like a million lightbulbs.

He cleared his throat. "I turned it off before I came over for dinner last night."

"And tonight?" she asked, wondering if his reasons for pushing her away had less to do with his feelings for her than the job he'd been hired to do. Somehow, that warmed her in places she'd been desperate to keep iced down. "Why didn't you reboot the cameras tonight?"

"I didn't have a chance after we discovered the cut brake line in your rental."

She heard the regret in his tense tone of voice. And the heat emanating from his powerful body flared hotter. "Great." His answer hadn't changed her gut reaction to his decision to keep what happened between them private. For all the right reasons, but still, she'd almost fallen for him. His admission gave her a great way to end things before she'd gotten too emotionally invested. "Just great. Now we won't know what that jerk did in my bedroom besides ransacking my stuff and stealing my wedding bands."

They continued watching the surveillance tape of her main living room and kitchen area. The person entered the space after an hour, carrying nothing.

"This doesn't make sense. Why break in if he didn't take anything except my rings?"

"What did you have in your computer files?"

"My recipes, the plans for my warehouse and expanding my distribution of my special marinades and sauces, but everyone I know that I'm close to already knows about my ideas."

"You have your laptop with you now?"

"Absolutely." She watched the person scan the room one more time, then open the door and leave. "No way would I leave it behind after what just happened. Plus, I need it to get my notes for the show tomorrow."

"You have it password protected?"

"Yes. My brother made sure I did. He's always loading firewalls and virus checkers and hacker protections on my computers."

"Get it. I want to check all your files. Make sure nothing's missing or..." he pushed a button on his laptop. "Added."

"Does this have anything to do with my brother? Whatever he's doing in Italy?"

"Could be. Not sure." He stood. "Get your laptop and we'll double check it for issues that shouldn't be there."

She made her way to the small foyer area in the cabin to retrieve her oversized crossbody bag. "Here," she said, handing him the laptop after returned to the table. "The password's *Love2CooknThyme32590.*"

He opened the screen, then keyed in the password. "We'll check the finder section first, look for anything out of place or missing."

She nodded, concern and anxiety filling her thoughts. If someone copied her secret recipes, she'd lose her first to enter in the market, the edge to stay ahead of the competition, possibly even future buyers. "So far all my folders look good. Click on that one." She pointed to the one labeled VATHYME as she shrugged off the blanket, no longer needing the comfort it brought her. Not when she had him sitting beside her.

"Okay, looks like your files are all intact. But there's something off."

# CHAPTER 10

"WHAT?" Reagan asked, adrenaline pinging through her veins and making her heart skip several beats.

"Looks like there's a backdoor code to let a person hack into the files from a remote location."

"So my files aren't protected?"

"Oh, they're not in danger of being stolen anymore." Brent keyed in some commands with his capable, large hands. "We must have interrupted the intruder before he could copy the files. I'll close the trapdoor, put up stronger firewall to prevent any further cyber-attacks."

Mesmerized, she watched him as he concentrated on continuing to key in more commands. God. Those hands brought another welcome thrill through her. Only a night ago, they'd held her, brought her to the edge of reason and given her amazing orgasms.

Reagan glanced away from the tapered fingers,

willed the electricity zapping into all her erogenous zones to fizzle out.

Failed.

"That should hold off the asshole," Brent said, pushing away from the table and leaning back with his arms folded behind his head.

"Good." Why did his muscles still tempt her, make her want to lick him all over? She shook off the desire to act on her impulse and wrapped the blanket around her shoulders again.

A wimpy physical barrier to the man's sheer masculine pheromone appeal, but it'd have to do if she wanted to keep her pride and self-respect intact. And her heart firmly out of the equation. "I should go to bed," she said, then stood.

He locked onto hers. "You going to be okay on your own?"

No, she mentally screamed. But she bit back the reply. If anyone had the skills to make it through a long, lonely night while processing a nightmare, she had them in quadruple digits. At least, she'd had them until Brent had come into her life. "Yes." She moved away from the table and from the delectable man sitting there. The sooner she got to bed, the better.

As she tucked the king-sized sheet and comforter around her, creating a cocoon she hoped would bring the rest she needed, Reagan heard Brent's heavy footfalls come closer to her door. A soft, oh so soft, brushing sound wafted into the room.

She recognized the noise of his head resting against the door separating them. Sighing, she snuggled deeper under the covers. How many nights had she heard that sound after she'd been widowed? The memories of her parents and her brother grappling with how to reach through the grief, the pain of her loss.

Sniffling, she swiped her eyes and gave up on the idea of attempting to sleep. She grabbed her e-reader and opened it to lose herself in the historical romance guaranteed to give her a happily-ever-after in lieu of getting one in real life.

The following morning, she arrived at Sadie Patterson's ranch with fatigue weighing her down and shadows so dark her stylist clucked in disapproval.

"I thought yesterday was bad enough," she said as she whipped a protective cape around Reagan's body. "But I'm going to have to pull out every trick I've got up my sleeve today to get you ready."

"I know. I'm sorry, but I have faith in your mad makeup skills."

"Girl, you're only going to be on air with two Hollywood stars that probably roll out of bed looking like they're at a movie debut and walking the red carpet."

"Too bad we're not filming at Al's Diner today," Reagan said as she surrendered to her stylist's ministrations.

"Girl, he could probably upstage you right now."

Reagan sighed. "Do your best," she said. "No one will care what I look like when they get a load of the sugar cookies and children's holiday recipe surprises we're making today."

Four hours later, after shooting the live show, Reagan slumped in one of the plush chairs located in her host's grand living room. "That went well," she said, glancing toward Sadie and Delaney's handsome husbands who stood next to the window facing the grand views outside.

Brent had his cell phone out and the two men nodded, faces grim. She didn't have to hear them to know the direction of their conversation.

"Here." Sadie set a cup of steaming cappuccino on the coffee table. "You look like you could use a double shot of this."

"Thanks," Reagan said, then lifted the cup and sipped gratefully. "Long night."

Both wives nodded. "We heard about the break-in," Delaney said. "I'm so sorry about the theft of your rings. That's got to hurt so bad."

She looked at her bare finger, realized the urge to twist them had long evaporated, but the love she'd had for her husband, the memories, remained. "Thanks, but I'm okay. And maybe they'll be recovered one day." Then she'd make something good come out of the bad and finally have the closure she needed to move on with her life. Alone, but free to love again. Just not Brent. She had to let him go. "I'm more concerned about the stalker. I can't figure out why anyone would come after me."

"If anyone can find out who is after you, it's those guys," Sadie said.

The scent of sugar cookies and sweet icing fondant mixtures still filled the air, but they didn't tempt her as much as Brent's powerful presence. "Yeah, I know, but I just wish…" She sipped the rich, creamy coffee again to swallow her confusion about her feelings for Brent. He'd given her the perfect reason to opt out of any permanent relationships with him, but a part of her rebelled. The selfish part, she sternly reminded herself.

"If it's any comfort," Sadie said softly. "From the way your bodyguard watches over you I think he's super attracted and you're radiating a mutual feeling. So he's definitely into you."

"Sure, and I can't control my reactions to him which only makes things worse."

"Why?" Delaney asked.

"I didn't actually know he'd been hired by my ding dong brother until yesterday." And she'd use that knowledge to keep the wedge between them until they returned to their respective lives. Apart.

"That's not good," Delaney said. "But it stinks because you clearly are still hot for each other."

"Doesn't matter," she said. "Even if I can find a way to forgive him for hiding the truth from me, he's got this weird protocol about not sleeping with his clients. Now that I'm officially one to him, I'm off-limits." A good thing if only her body would cooperate with her reasoning.

Sadie and Delaney snorted in a very un-star like way. "Oh, that's so rich given he's already broken that idiotic rule," Delaney said.

"Yeah. These macho dudes act all tough and pretend they can't be with us but that wasn't a problem with our Brotherhood Protectors," Sadie added before lifting one of the holiday cookies from the plate on the table and taking a bite.

"Yeah." Delaney caressed her belly bump. "Protocol, schmotocol."

A sudden, sharp need lanced through Reagan. Old losses mingled with the current crappy feelings swirling in her brain. "The thing is we can't give each other what we really want. Plus you both knew what and who your guys were before you slept with them."

Both women looked toward Brent, then back to Reagan. "Well, if I know men, and trust me with three brothers I've got a good handle on them. I bet Brent figured your brother hired him, so you didn't officially become a client in his brain until an actual threat surfaced," Delaney asked. "And, if nothing turned up, I am also willing to bet he'd want to take this to a whole new level, see where your attraction leads."

Reagan flushed hot. "Too bad a threat surfaced.

Now everything is all messed up," she said, though she had her own secret too. One she didn't have to reveal now, and she could let him go despite the fierce longing in her heart for him. For more. For a different ending. "I don't know whether to thank my brother or kick him in the gonads the next time I see him. I guess I'll have to tolerate an *I tried to stop you* lecture after I arrive in Tuscany. Ugh" Her next trip to Italy had been booked to coincide with his and Isabella's first child's arrival.

"Can't blame you for dreading that confrontation given my own brothers constantly interfering with my life before I married Ethan. But what about later?" Delaney asked. "After this is over and you're back in Virginia? Any way you'll give him a second chance?"

Nope. Not going to happen. Not when Brent's admission had given her a reason to end things with a nice, neat *see you later now that you're not guarding me* sayonara. "His pulling back, treating me like a client, is really for the best." She grabbed a cookie and took a healthy bite. Though the flavor was perfection on her tongue, bitterness slipped down her throat.

"Are you sure you because everything in your face says you still want him," Delaney said.

"Maybe, but he's a covert operative in some secret agency that puts him in dangerous situations all the time. He told me this was supposed to be an easy job. Kind of like a vacation," she said, still struggling to reconcile his career with the realities she'd faced after losing her husband. She couldn't give him what Brent ultimately wanted, and she didn't dare risk her heart for a man who put himself in the line of fire on a regular basis. "I'm certain most of his missions aren't always so easy or safe." And safe was what she wanted. Alone and single and free. Right? No worries about losing someone she loved again. Double right? No pressures about making babies and creating families. Triple right? So why did she have to go and have all these feelings for the wrong kind of man altogether?

She glanced his way again, caught his eyes with hers. Those whiskey-colored eyes that had once darkened with lust for her. Even now, the pupils went black as night, but Reagan averted her gaze, breaking the slender thread of contact.

She didn't doubt the lust, the attraction. But she seriously doubted how they could move forward from this point without either of them getting hurt. Would she have slept with him had she known the truth all along? Despite the longing, the desire pinging between them, could she have been with him knowing the danger that shadowed his life on a daily basis?

She didn't know. And she didn't know if she dared to examine her own fears too closely. Not when they no longer had anything to bind them together other than Brent protecting her from some asshole trying to rob her of the one thing she could count on. Herself. And her own dreams.

"YOU GET the new intel about the rest of the show's crew?" Hank Patterson asked after taking a tug off his craft beer bottle.

A fire crackled in the living room's corner, scenting the room with wood smoke. Though Hank's ranch home was warm and inviting, every muscle in Brent's body remained coiled. And the case only contributed part of the tension. "Yes. Nothing has changed since the background checks I ran before I arrived at Eagle Point." Brent pinched the bridge of his nose, stared at the pristine white blanket of snow covering the land surrounding the ranch. "Owen Davidson left yesterday. Back to New York to get ready for his grand opening on New Year's Eve." And he'd been tethered to Montana, sticking to his original assignment to guard Reagan.

"That puts him at the bottom of your suspect list," Ethan Walker said.

The flamboyant chef had barely scratched the edge of Brent's mental radar screen, given he'd left the Eagle Point well before the break-in. Still, Brent never took anything for granted. He couldn't afford to take those kinds of chances with a client. "Doesn't mean he's off it yet," he said grimly. Only he couldn't pursue his suspicions other than run deeper background checks while keeping Reagan alive.

"He didn't drive the SUV that crashed last week," Hank reminded him.

"True, but I contacted one of CRUSH's top operatives to follow up to make sure his story holds while Reagan filmed *Cooking Thyme* today." He returned his attention to the men standing with him. "Tori's stationed in New York until she has her baby, but she's continuing to supervise undercover ops. She'll assign an agent to tail Owen while we're in Montana and update me if anything raises a red flag." Meanwhile, he'd check out a few other leads and pass the info on to Hank's team for backup.

"Good plan," Hank said. "You want me to send reinforcements to the ranch until the show wraps?"

"Extra eyes would be great, but I don't want to tip off anyone who has it in for Reagan."

"I've got a couple of new recruits to offer additional protection."

"My agency will cover the costs."

"Ben Lawson is more than your commander, he's my friend and Ethan's brother-in-law." Hank held up a hand to stop any argument. "Consider this a favor. If you need any additional equipment, give me the heads up and we'll make sure you get the supplies pronto."

"Thanks." The hairs on the back of his neck raised and Brent turned toward the three women sitting in the great room. If looks could kill, those three sets of eyes had definitely speared him. "Better get going. Reagan's exhausted and there are more shows to film before the new year."

"Sleigh ride segment staying on the agenda?" Hank asked.

"Affirmative. Not that I'm happy about it, but we're sticking to the game plan. I want to draw out the bastard who's after her." Brent flexed his fingers, then fisted them. "Can't do that if we wrap her in bubble wrap."

"She tell you that?" Ethan asked with a hint of humor in his voice.

"In a nutshell. Woman's too stubborn for her own good."

"She's in good company," Hank said. "And if she's as strong as our wives, then you've got the best person to support your effort to catch the person fucking with her life."

A slight heaviness settled in his chest. A part of Brent wanted to ask the men standing next to him how they'd survived the experience of having the women they loved in jeopardy. Another ping of pain hit him behind the breastbone. Had he gone and fallen in love with Reagan? Too soon to tell. Still, where could all lead if he acted on the emotion connection he'd experienced with her? Been 100% honest before he'd slept with her too?

Where the brotherhood protectors were

concerned, their answers were given by the lives they led today. Each had become husbands, happily married, with babies, children. Families filled with love and acceptance. And running their ongoing business of protecting the innocent, stopping crimes and more.

"We've got a cover story for the next week. Figured we already hooked up once, so everyone still thinks we're dating." Fake dating instead of the real thing, but the best way to make his constant presence in her world believable now. Once again, the idea of leaving the off-site investigating to the agents in the field ate at his gut, but his hands were tied.

Still, now he wondered again if he could have had everything the men standing next to him had today with Reagan if he hadn't completely screwed up his chance to have her in his life on a permanent basis? From the flash of fire he saw in her blue eyes before she looked away, he doubted he'd ever have another opportunity to prove himself to her.

"You got it bad," Ethan said softly, cutting into Brent's jumbling, confusing thoughts.

"Yeah, but I fucked up."

"Give her time. She'll come around."

"No. I don't think she will," Brent said. "She went through hell after her husband died. Now she doubts everything that happened between us before I had to tell her the truth."

"Whoa. You did blow it."

Brent scraped his fingers through his hair. "Royally."

"We've been there," Ethan said. "Just hang in and you'll figure out how to get through to her."

"Right now I'm focusing on protecting her. Period." And alive. How to reach past her guard... how to show Reagan he wanted to see where the heat and the fire flaring between them would lead would have to wait.

But time was running out. Not only would the filming wrap up in less than a week which would mean her returning home, someone out there wanted her out of the way before she caught that flight out of Bozeman. If that person didn't succeed, her life was in jeopardy. Then he'd lose... fuck. He'd lose the only woman he wanted to have a chance at a normal life again.

At least one where a family didn't disintegrate when the glue holding the fabric together evaporated. Trusting Reagan to stick, to be that person, meant trusting her with more than he'd been willing to give to others in the past.

He'd forgotten how to be the kind of person who could give himself 100 percent to another. But Reagan had unlocked something deep in him. And he didn't want to let her go.

## CHAPTER 11

THE SUN'S waning rays danced color on the horizon, decorating the sky with brilliant oranges and hues of pink onto the whisper thin clouds. Reagan shivered as the air grew colder in the early evening hour and yet she kept herself away from Brent's comforting heat, choosing to sit opposite him on the sleigh. No way would she give her hormones a chance to override her resolve to let this fledgling relationship fly out of her brain. The stakes were too high for both of them.

Eric carried a stash of brightly colored blankets in hues of red, green, purples and golds to the sleigh and loaded them inside. "Here," he said. "These should keep everyone warm while we ride out to the ranch's bonfire location."

"Thanks." Reagan reached for one and accidentally brushed Brent's gloved hand. A jolt of electricity, intense awareness, zipped through her. Not good. Not good at all. "I've got this." She gripped the blanket and scooted to the front of the sleigh, then wrapped the folds around her.

A team of draft horses had already been hitched to the front and the driver sat in front on a special platform. Behind her, *Cooking Thyme's* film crew rode in a flatbed truck to get the footage. Today wouldn't be completely live. The sleigh ride would be spliced in before they uploaded the show to the At Home Network channel.

The driver called to the horses, a merry jingle of bells chimed in tandem with his orders to giddy up. The sleigh pitched into motion and she tucked the gold blanket around her legs, hunkering down while trying to look like she actually enjoyed the frosty, cold weather as they skimmed over the packed snow trail.

"Smile," Angela called. "And snuggle in with that handsome guy. It'll make the audience wonder about your relationship."

Her muscles tensed, knotted at the base of her neck. She tugged her scarf and squeezed the ends. The last person she wanted to snuggle in with was Brent. But she didn't have a choice. Their entire set up to drive out the person who'd been stalking her meant staying together. Something she couldn't allow to sway her determination to keep her distance.

She pasted a not-so-fake smile onto her face as Brent shifted to her side of the sleigh and wrapped his arm around her shoulders, drawing her close. The scent of leather and man wafted around her and her mouth watered despite her internal resolve to keep him at mental arm's length.

But her hyperactive hormones continued to betray her in all the wrong ways. Sighing inwardly, she allowed herself to take advantage of his hot, sexy as sin body.

"Perfect," her director called from the truck. "Okay, let's get some wide angle shots of the sleigh as it glides over the snow, then we'll cut to the bonfire cookout."

"Sounds good." She searched the area whizzing by them. "Do you see anything out of the ordinary?"

"No. Doesn't mean there isn't someone out there waiting to hurt you," he said, tightening his grip.

She could hear Brent's steady breathing as they rode over the trail. His calm demeanor gave her a measure of peace of mind. Oh, how she wished the circumstances bringing them together had been different. But even then... if wishes were horses, she'd have an entire stable. "I just want this to be over." And for Brent to go back to his life so she could resume hers.

After riding for an hour without incident, they arrived at the ranch's bonfire site. Night had completely fallen, but the bonfire's flames and the candles flickering in strategic places all around the circle of Adirondack chairs and logs and rustic, tree core topped tables lit the space.

"The prep station's ready," Eric said when he reached the sleigh. "You've got everything you need to make your perfect campfire meal."

Reagan took her assistant's gloved hand and exited the sleigh as Brent hopped out to stand beside her. She made her way to the long table located behind a row of chairs and tables. A holiday linen cloth with a festive poinsettia and silver bell print covered the length. Her breath bottled in her lungs. The decorative fabric reminded her too much about the oversized poinsettia Brent had given her two days earlier as part of his so-called apology.

*Focus on the meal, not the man. Period. Nothing else matters. And don't think about who might be out there trying to do God knows what.* She moved past the long branches that had been carved into points to spear marshmallows for the traditional s'mores and over to the oranges. Most had already been prepped by the show's staff, but she'd get filmed while she completed cutting off the tops and hollowing the pulp out before she inserted the chocolate, marshmallows and, in some, Grand Marnier.

"You did a great job laying out the sequence of food we're using today," she said to her assistant.

"Thanks," Eric said, pouring hot spiced cider into

mugs, then adding cinnamon sticks to them. "Here. This'll keep you warm."

"So will the studio lights." The heat radiating from the equipment made the temperature comfortable enough to take off her gloves before she clasped the mug.

She glanced toward the two men who'd ridden to the site with her crew. They'd positioned themselves on opposite sides of the perimeter while Brent continued to stay up close and personal with her. Though the men had behaved like tourists on a vacation and excited to see the show, she understood their role as additional security.

She gritted her teeth, forced herself to drink the aromatic cider to calm herself. How did A-list celebrities deal with the constant presence of other people around them? She didn't mind being with her crew, but this additional security made her skin crawl. She felt like a tiny ant under a microscope.

She shook off the thought, turning her attention toward the audience that had arrived in other sleighs and on snowmobiles.

"Okay, let's get this party started," her director said, then Angela turned to Eric and passed him a clipboard. "I want you to takeover filming after the second commercial break."

"Really?"

"Of course," she said. "You did an excellent job while I recuperated from the crash. You deserve to do more than pour cider and give people their scripts."

"Thanks. I promise I won't screw this up," Eric said, his grin beaming so bright, the lights reflected off his teeth.

"Brent, we'll want you front and center for the tasting," Angela continued.

"Can't wait," he said.

His voice, deep and as panty melting as ever sent tingles through her. She willed the instant attraction to the sensual sound, one she'd heard throughout an entire night of wild, crazy sexy times, back into the do-not-go-there-zone.

"All right." She pointed to one of the Adirondack chairs placed around the bonfire pit. "Take a seat and we'll get started."

He didn't go to where she indicated. Instead, he walked his way too hot ass to the opposite side of the table. "I'll stand here so I can get first bites of everything."

And so he could continue guarding her while pretending he didn't want her anymore. "Fine. Do it your way," she said, then she welcomed the rest of her audience to the makeshift set. Reagan transformed into show host and went about preparing her holiday campfire meal for the mixture of people drawn from the ranch's guests and employees.

While she prepped, cooked and chatted with the audience, the bonfire's flames rose into the ebony night sky. The staff continued to feed the fire, sparks danced and wove into the air as the wood crackled, snapped. By the time Reagan had pulled the last, yummy orange boat filled with marshmallows, chocolate and Grand Marnier for the adults from the fire, satisfied sighs, and murmurs of approval floated around her.

Clapping, Angela called, "That's a wrap."

After they cleaned the set and cleared the area, Brent walked her back to the sleigh. "That was amazing. You really do know how to pull together great dishes that anyone can learn to make."

"I like food to be accessible, easy to prep. A lot of people are intimidated by frou-frou recipes."

"I'll have to make this stuff for my nieces and nephews," he said as they settled into the sleigh's seats once more.

Pain lanced behind her breastbone and her stomach coiled into a massive knot. Pressing her palm against her belly, she scooted away from him. Once more, he reminded her about his family. Something she could never give him. Even more reason to use his original reason to hang out with her, the subterfuge, to drive him out of her mind, her life.

SNOWMOBILES ROARED in the distance while the horses drew the Brent and Reagan back to Eagle

Point Ranch. He draped his arm casually around her stiff shoulders, refusing to let her push him away. "Won't be long before we're back," he said. "Relax. Let me do the worrying for you."

"Easier said than done."

"I know," he said. "Whoever rifled through your cabin and caused the accidents, cut the brake line, is still out there." No one had surfaced today and, according to his CRUSH contact in New York, Owen Davidson had been seen entering his penthouse in Manhattan. The news had struck the chef off his list of suspects. But that meant Brent didn't have much left to go on.

Once they got back to the resort's main lodge, he'd continue to run background checks and go over the findings Hank's security experts discovered. Look for more links and connections.

Her director had checked out. Even now, her entire focus was on the show. The flatbed truck drove behind them at a slow crawl and she directed another scene to splice into the show's rolling credits before they'd upload the final video to the network.

Other than the biting wind slapping the sides of the sleigh, nothing seemed out of place. But danger had a way of lurking in the shadows. He heard her teeth clattering. "Here." He lifted another blanket from the stash placed on the bench seat beside them. "Tuck in."

She withdrew from his embrace long enough to

fold the additional covering around her upper body. "What will we do if we can't find the jerk who's stalking me?"

How much could he tell her about the secret agency he worked for and closely tied her family was to it? Not much. Not unless the agency's commander okayed him to do so. "Your brother has contacts in Virginia," he said after a beat of silence while scanning the surrounding trees for any movement.

A loud crack sounded. Suddenly, the sleigh listed to the left and the horses continued trotting as the driver called for them to halt.

"Get down." He brought Reagan to the floor and, while shielding her body, he withdrew his gun, cocked it to load the first bullet. "Stay here."

"Their harness collar snapped," the driver said, pulling the reins.

The horses loped ahead as the flatbed truck behind came to a halt, barely missing the back of the sleigh. More shouts, orders to get down sounded from the brotherhood protector guards in the vehicle.

The sleigh skidded to a stop and the driver twisted around. "I'll check the chains and riggings," he said. "But you'll have to finish this ride back to the ranch in the truck."

Another noise, tell-tale buzz of bullets zipping through the pristine night air, sounded. "Fuck the ride back," Brent called, still covering Reagan's body.

"We've got to find the bastard who's taking pot shots at us."

"On it," one of the men Hank sent called before ordering the rest of the crew to stay low.

Both Brotherhood Protectors slinked out of the flatbed truck and positioned themselves behind the side, already geared up with infrared goggles and their weapons out.

Adrenaline shot through him, every muscle ready to spring into action. But his primary mission meant remaining pat. A bullet struck the sleigh's side. The driver had already dropped and rolled under the now prone sleigh.

"You packing?" Brent asked the driver.

"Always. Never know what kind of animal could turn up."

"Good. Reagan do exactly as I say. Got it?"

"Yes."

"We crawl together to the edge," he said. "Hank's men will give us cover until we can get you to the truck. Once you're inside, drop to the floorboard and stay there until I give the all clear."

"Brent. I'm scared."

"You have every right to be afraid, but I won't let anything happen to you. You're too important to me." There, he said it. What she did with the revelation after he caught the bastard attacking them, remained unclear.

That she didn't counter his statement or give him

a cold shoulder rivaling the frigid mountain air, gave him a measure of hope.

But first, he had to save her.

And the Bluetooth hearing devices they used to communicate with the other bodyguards had sketchy connections. The cell towers were unreliable on a good day. The wind had kicked up another storm, clouds billowed overhead, and he could smell the scent of impending snowfall.

Relying on hand signals, he communicated his plans to the men at the truck. One nodded, tilted his head to the front wheel. Then, with another round of bullets flying around them, he slowly brought Reagan to the sleigh's exit point. One Brotherhood Protector held the handle to the truck's passenger door, tilted his head toward the metal frame.

Brent inhaled a sharp breath, the air misting when he released it. "We crawl over now."

"Okay."

Her voice trembled, but she held his gaze with confident eyes. As he moved them out of the back, then crawled toward the first man beside the truck, keeping their bodies low to the ground. Overhead, another shot rang, but the extra guards returned fire and slipped the door open.

"Get in." Brent covered her back with his, facing outward, his gun ready.

More shots rang out, pinged on the opposite side of the vehicle as she moved into the vehicle's cavity.

He scoped out a shadow moving in the trees. Whoever had been shooting had help. Before he could call out a warning, he felt the sting of a bullet entering his left thigh just as the door slammed behind him.

He dropped to the ground, rolled under the chassis, and shouted, "There's another gunman out there."

## CHAPTER 12

REAGAN'S HEART RACED, she tasted acid and bile sloshed in her belly. The scent of blood filled the air as she hunkered at the bottom of the passenger seats with Eric and Angela.

"Thank God you're okay," Angela whispered. "Who the hell is doing this to us?"

"I don't know," Reagan said. "But Brent's been protecting me ever since I arrived at Eagle Point."

"Were you threatened before you came here?" Eric asked, his face as white as the snow falling outside.

"No. But my brother…" She swallowed down the sick feeling rising in her throat as memories of another blood bath surged. "He didn't want me to do the live shows. I guess he was right to hire Brent, but I sure wish he'd told me." Then she wouldn't have hopped into the sack with Brent like a giddy schoolgirl or, even better, she'd have gone into the affair with her eyes wide open and her heart barricaded with steel.

And now he could be dead because he'd protected her.

Another man giving up his life, so she could live. Renewed guilt flooded her brain, making her eyes swim with unshed tears. "If he dies, I..."

"You can't blame yourself." Her director moved closer and together, the three held on to each other while a flurry of shouting and gunfire cut through the night air.

Beneath the floorboard, hidden from her view, the man she'd grown to like way too much for her own good lay bleeding. A razor like sensation scraped the inside of her throat. Old wounds, self-recriminations, flared through her nerves. She edged back toward the door and pressed down the handle.

"Where the hell do you think you're going?" Eric demanded.

"I have to try to save Brent. I won't let another person die because of me," Reagan said after several tense seconds. "I can't live through that again." Then she carefully opened the latched door and half-crawled out of the truck to crouch beside the back wheel.

She peered under the chassis, didn't see Brent. Her heart thudded dully in her ears as she registered the blood smearing the ground amidst the telltale signs of handprints showing how he'd dragged himself out.

And footprints. Adrenaline pinged like a thousand pricks over her skin, raising every hair on her body. Quickly, she turned to check the surrounding area. The sound of gunfire had moved into the trees beyond the truck and she heard Brent's voice before she saw another familiar shape come into view.

Owen Davidson stepped out of the woods with a gun in his hand with the barrel trained directly on her. "Don't make another move or I'll shoot her," he said calmly as he walked toward Reagan.

Behind him, just to the left, she spotted Brent propped against an evergreen pine. He shook his head, warning her to keep her gaze away from him and on Owen.

She glanced back at her former competitor as the wind swirled snow around her, slapped against her body and cheeks.

But the frigid air seemed positively like island paradise hot compared to the Owen's cold, icy gray stare. "Why?" she asked through chattering lips. "I thought we were friends."

"You thought wrong." Owen closed the remaining distance between them, standing within a foot of her. "Stand up," he said, jostling his weapon toward her.

"You're supposed to be in New York," she said, obeying his command. "How did you get back so fast?"

"I never left."

"But someone saw you arrive home," she said.

"They saw a decoy. Someone I hired months ago to play a part for me. He's a dead ringer."

Another movement behind him distracted her. Brent making his way over to another stand of trees located perpendicularly to the truck.

Sweat beaded on her forehead despite the cold, winter air. She couldn't let Owen figure out that she still had an ace up her sleeve. But she'd have to play every card trick she had in her arsenal to win this deadly game.

"You always were an excellent planner," she said, mustering a calm facade. "Doesn't mean I know why you'd do this to me."

"Couple of reasons. One. I deserved to win and two." He held the gun higher. "I needed the prize money for my restaurants when I did."

More heat flashed behind her ribs, bringing another wash of sweat into her extremities. Confusion warred with the panic still pinging along her nerves. "You're one of the top chefs in New York," she said, keeping her entire focus on him though she continued to see movement in the trees with her peripheral vision. She had to keep Owen talking to give Brent time to get to her. "That doesn't make sense."

"Yes. I am. I should have won that fucking competition."

Not according to the viewers and Angela. Angela and the rest of the crew wanted her because she was relatable, accessible to the audience they were targeting. Plus she had a compelling story of overcoming a major tragedy and doing better than surviving. She saved her parents' restaurant during lean economic times with innovative, accessible recipes. She brought a wealth of life experiences to the table that Owen could never bring. Still, she tamped down the rage boiling in her cells.

"You're definitely a better cook than me." She hugged her waist, acted like she was cold and slipped her hands inside her pockets. After what had happened in the cabin, she'd begun carrying a concealed surprise as extra backup. "I agree," Reagan said, wrapping her hand around the portable mace. Now she only needed to catch the bastard off guard and get close enough to make the stuff effective in bringing him down.

"What you think doesn't matter anymore."

The howling wind made talking difficult, but it also concealed Brent's steady approach from the rear toward Owen. "Why not? If it's the show you want, then I'll step aside." Not really, but she'd say anything to keep this jerk's monster sized ego happy at this point.

"Your offer is about a year too late." He waved the gun a bit wildly. "Frankly, you stole that show from me. If that hadn't happened, I wouldn't have needed to get the loan from that money shark. So you have no one to blame for this but yourself."

Anger bubbled inside her. She'd been blaming herself for a lot of things, but this shithead didn't deserve to win the show at all. "Why is it too late? You could just get the money now. Plus, you stole my wedding bands. Why? To hock them for more money?" She popped the top off the can she held, still hiding it from view.

He sneered. "Those rings couldn't come close to covering my losses."

"Then why'd you steal them? They meant nothing to you."

"Those fucking rings bought you the show," he said, waving the gun again. "Every time you twisted those bands around your finger, you got the audience's attention. They bought your pity me act hook, line and sinker."

Anger resurfaced when she registered his vile, vindictive words. The bastard had no concept of loss, grief. But she didn't show her disgust, knowing the stakes facing her. And Brent. "If you're so broke, how'd you fund this crazy operation?"

"After I got myself in over my head with my expansions, I ran into trouble with a loan shark and he offered me a deal I couldn't resist."

She swallowed down the renewed acid in her throat. "What kind of deal?"

"Turns out your brother killed the wrong man

when he busted that cartel in Virginia. That guy had connections to a terrorist group that depended on the funds the heroin would bring them. So… an eye for an eye and all that jazz." He raised the gun, cocked the trigger. "I get out of debt and a debt is repaid with your blood."

BRENT HAD ONE SHOT REMAINING. Thankfully, Reagan had kept the idiot talking long enough to give him time to get within reach of making a direct hit. Still, a part of him wanted to strangle her for leaving the safety of the truck's interior cabin.

But time had run out. He fired his weapon as Reagan rushed Owen and sprayed the bastard with mace before diving to grab the weapon the jerk released. Owen dropped to his knees, clutching his face with one hand as the mace worked its magic on him, burning his eyes. The other he had on his side, holding back the flow of blood from the bullet wound.

"Bitch." He flailed his arms and struck Reagan before she could reach the weapon. "You fucking bitch."

"You haven't seen anything yet," she yelled, kicking him in the chest. "Never mess with a former tomboy, asshole."

Brent ignored the shooting pain in his thigh, the

pressure of the tourniquet he'd belted around it earlier stemming the flow of blood. Sheets of sleet mingled with the snow swirling around him. He raced to Owen who crouched on the ground, groping for the gun and screaming curses.

He tackled the bleeding man. "Get the gun," he yelled to Reagan. "Then get back to the truck."

"Got it."

Owen twisted out of Brent's grip, lunged for Reagan and caught one ankle, tripping her. "You're not going anywhere." He punched her legs, her back, but she scissor-kicked her way out of his pummeling hands.

White hot heat blazed behind Brent's breast-bone, propelling him forward to wrestle Owen away from her. Holding him in a headlock, he pinned the man to the ground with his knee. He reached for the plastic tie grips in his pocket and tossed a pair to Reagan. "Secure his ankles. I'll get his wrists."

She knelt and locked the flailing legs together. "Where are the other men?" she asked.

"One's down, but still alive. The other's got the second shooter locked down until reinforcements arrive."

Snowmobiles engines roared in the distance, the sounds echoing closer as they came into view. Within minutes, they circled the broken sleigh, truck and sleigh driver, who had the horses under control. One man levered off a still idling machine and walked toward them.

"Good thing the damned cell phone towers kicked into gear before this mess blew in off the mountain," Hank Patterson said as he kneeled next to Brent. "He's got some serious injuries."

"He'll survive long enough to go to trial and spend a time in prison." Brent had no sympathy for the coward whimpering beneath his knee. "You got transportation lined up to get this asshole and your man to the hospital in Bozeman?"

"Yep," Hank said, then turned to one of his men. "Get the medics here to load this guy into one of the rescue toboggans."

"Will do."

Brent switched places with the Brotherhood Protector, letting him take care of the man he'd captured. Then, he tried to stand, only to collapse to the ground again.

"Brent." Reagan knelt beside him, cradled his head, then looked at Hank. "They shot him in the leg. I think it's a lot worse than he's letting on."

Hank joined her, waved to another man carrying a medical bag. "Doctor will take a look at him. Make sure he's okay."

The doctor rushed over and, after examining Brent's injury, said, "That's one nasty wound you've got there. Most likely the bullet punctured an artery."

"Do you have enough rescue toboggans to get him out of here?" Reagan asked, her voice wavering.

Hank shook his head. "He'll have to ride to the ranch in the truck." He indicated toward the sleigh driver. "Snag all the blankets and we'll settle him in the back."

"I'm riding with him."

His breath temporarily bottled in his chest and a floating sensation permeated through his fuzzy brain. Maybe she hadn't completely kicked him out of her heart. "You'll freeze," Brent said, black spots entering his vision.

"I'm the reason you're hurt. There's no way I'm leaving you alone."

"You'll need to get med-evacuated along with other men after we get to Eagle Point Ranch," the doctor said. "I'd ride with him, but your man is in grave danger."

"Understood," Hank said. "Let's get him loaded before the storm cuts off our route to the ranch."

Two more of Hank's men lifted Brent and carried him to the truck. After loading the back with blankets and activating thermal heating packs, they drove through the storm to head back to the ranch.

She got down beside Brent, held him, lending him her body heat. The warmth she offered and the gleam in her gaze brought another surge of hope into his veins. Maybe he did have a chance with Reagan after all. "I'm sorry I didn't tell you about why I was here right away," he said. "You're so much more than a client and guarding you meant protecting a possible future together too."

Her beautiful blue eyes swam with tears. "You were just carrying out orders," she said. "I forgive you, but we can't worry about the future yet. Just focus on getting better."

A niggle of doubt wove through him. She forgave him, but why wouldn't she go to the next level? Before he could ask her to give him another chance or if he even had one with her, his vision blurred, and he struggled to maintain consciousness.

"Reagan, stay with me."

"I'm not leaving until I know you're okay," she whispered against his mouth, tears tracking down her wind slapped cheeks, the drops ice cold as they landed on his face.

"If you really do forgive me, then know that I will do everything in my power to prove you made the right decision to stick with me. Maybe we can have the family we want one day too."

She inhaled a shuddering breath, swiped the tears tracking down her face away. "You'll have everything you deserve, but…"

His vision blurred before she could finish speaking and then everything went black.

# CHAPTER 13

THOUGH BRENT'S words warmed her more than any blanket or thermal pack, Reagan's veins still ran cold. She feared his injury could kill him, but even worse, she hadn't told him everything he needed to know about her. About the family she couldn't give him.

She'd wait until he got through this ordeal before she told him why she couldn't be with him in a permanent way. Not just because of his job, but because she couldn't give him the future he craved.

After arriving at the ranch, then enduring the helicopter ride to Bozeman's City Hospital, she paced the floor in the waiting room. "What's taking so long?" she asked Delaney.

"It's only been an hour. Half that time is prep for surgery. Don't worry," Delaney said reassuringly. "He's going to be fine. Then you can move forward."

Delaney had already given her some information about Brent's line of work after she'd contacted her brother Ben in California with the news. "He'll just go on another secret mission," she said. "I'm not the right woman for him." And that's the excuse she'd clung to for several days after he'd revealed the truth to her about why he'd turned up at Eagle Point. But her secret weighed in more heavily on her decision to let him go.

"Life is messy, but you know better than anyone that it doesn't come with a guarantee," Delaney said.

"True." After all, her husband had been an insurance adjuster and he'd died almost instantly in a crazy hit and run crash. Now she knew the truth. No one was to blame for his death except the drug dealer her brother had chased through the Virginia mountains on that fateful day.

"At least I know what Colton's really doing in Italy." His wife's winery had been transformed into another secret headquarters for Covert Rescuers' Undercover Shield and he commanded the European branch.

And she'd learned that from her friend in Virginia. That Saxon Vineyards owner and operator, Alexandra Saxon, commanded an entire underground secret agency fighting for justice still blew Reagan's mind.

Now, despite discovering everything she'd been

cleared to know, she still had to make one of the toughest decisions of her life. She couldn't choose to stay with Brent and see where this thing between them was going. Not without depriving him of a family too.

She'd already fallen half in love him and she hadn't factored that into her life plans. Letting him go wouldn't be easy, but she'd survived worse.

So, when she walked into the recovery room to see him for the first time, she made her final decision. Taking the seat beside his bed, she took his hand and held it. "How do you feel?" she asked.

"Like I got hit by a train," he said, his voice gravelly.

"Here," she said. "Drink this." She raised the water cup the nurse had left for him to sip on.

After he finished drinking. He held her eyes with those sexy, whiskey-colored eyes. "Thanks for staying. For giving me another chance."

She squeezed her eyes shut, then opened them after a long pause. Why did saying goodbye to this man hurt so much? "I don't regret being with you, but Brent, this thing between us can't go anywhere. Not really."

"Why not? Other agents get married, have families. I know there's a danger element, and you've suffered a lot after your husband died, but I'm pretty motivated to stay alive."

She wrapped her shoulders with determination.

"Yes, I did. But I didn't just lose my husband in the crash," she said. "I lost my baby."

He sat straighter despite the IV hooked to his arm and reached for her. "God. I'm sorry. I am."

Reagan didn't let him touch her. Couldn't or she'd falter. "So am I. But I've got a good life now. The show. My restaurant. Friends."

"You could have more. You could have me. There's no reason you can't have a family one day." He gripped her hand. "Reagan. You're the first woman who's touched me in places I forgot I still had. You made me come alive again. There's no reason why we can't try to make a family if this heat, attraction… this need between us leads to something more."

"I wish I could tell you yes, let's go for it, but I can't," she said, choking back tears. "My injuries were so severe that when I miscarried, my parts took a beating. I had a partial hysterectomy. I can't get pregnant, let alone carry a child to term. I refuse to let you get involved with me when you clearly want children. I won't deprive you of that."

Then, with the truth finally out, she released his hand and stood. "I'm not going to lie. This is hard for me, but I believe I'm making the right decision for both of us."

She turned, heard Brent call her name, but she didn't look back. No. She had to move forward and live the life she had recreated for herself in order to give them both a chance at a better future.

LESS THAN TWO WEEKS LATER, Reagan gathered her catering supplies and loaded them into her van. "We're running ahead of schedule," she said to her assistant.

"That's because you've been working non-stop ever since you left the hospital room in Bozeman," Eric said. "Face it. You're using your job to run away from your feelings."

"I'm just focused, trying to make my new line of sauces a hit on the market," she said, refusing to admit the truth to Eric. But deep down, she ached.

Sure, she'd renewed her contract with the At Home Network and her plans to expand her special marinades and sauces were slowly coming together. A warehouse had been procured, people hired to make the additional batches of sauces, and a marketing schedule was on tap for the following month.

And between wrapping up the live filming of the show, operating the restaurant and catering company, she hadn't slowed down since returning to Magnolia Falls.

"Whatever you say," Eric said, shutting the van's

back doors. "But those shadows under your eyes aren't going anywhere soon."

"Button it," she said, then made her way to the passenger side and stepped inside. "Just drive."

"Gotten a lot grumpier too." Eric started the engine. "Good thing you're a pro and the fans haven't picked up on your perpetually lousy mood."

Driving down the highway toward Saxon Vineyards, Reagan gazed through the window at the passing winter wonderland. She thought she'd made the right decision by leaving Brent. But ever since she'd walked out of that hospital room, nothing had been the same.

All the things that had once brought her joy had evaporated. Even cooking, running the catering business, everything. All her plans coming to fruition and everything right on schedule for a spring rollout of her sauces.

The show on the At Home Network was a hit. The fans craved even more after what had happened in Montana.

A deer with large antlers loped in the trees they drove beside and then disappeared into the wilderness. Once more, an emptiness settled behind her breastbone that she couldn't fill. She'd been there before, believed she'd never overcome the true hollow feeling she'd experienced after she'd lost her husband and the pregnancy.

But then, someone had come along who'd refilled

that gaping wound. And that someone had been Brent.

She'd used her career and her past to protect herself from losing someone she cared about again. And she'd been too quick to push him out of her life, especially after he'd apologized and come clean about his career, everything that had brought him into her world.

A dullness in her chest along with the invisible press of an anchor on her shoulders weighed heavy. She'd made a gargantuan mistake when she left him alone in that hospital room and had given up another shot at having the life she'd missed for years. A life with someone who stood by her, loved her. How could she have done that to herself? To him?

A surge of energy bolted through her as the winter sun glared through the van's front window. She'd never even given Brent the chance to show how much he cared after revealing her secret. Running away would no longer be how she coped with her losses. No. She'd face them head-on.

"You know what, Eric?" She turned to her assistant as they cruised into the vineyard's road. "You're right. I am hiding behind my pots and pans to avoid facing something really difficult. But that ends today." Somehow, she'd use her connection to Alexandra and her vast secret agency's network to track down Brent. Then she'd go to him as soon as humanly possible to apologize for being such a dope.

If he truly cared about her, he'd accept her without condition. She'd known that all along, before and after his shocking revelation in Montana.

So Reagan would reach out to her friend while catering Saxon Vineyard's annual New Year's Eve Gala. Find out where to find Brent and take the first steps to giving them another shot.

If he'd take her back.

But, as they arrived at the vineyard's beautiful old world chateau style manor's parking lot, a familiar Stetson hat came into view.

Her heart skipped, bounced against her sternum. Adrenaline zipped through her veins and her fingertips tingled as a humming buzzed in her ears. "Stop," she said, unbuckling her seatbelt with shaking hands. "I've got to get out now."

Eric braked, and she rushed out of the van, calling Brent's name. He turned and locked eyes with her and everything she missed rushed back into her mind, her heart. Her soul.

"What are you doing in Magnolia Falls?" she asked, making her way toward him.

"I transferred here after I got out of the hospital."

Her breath caught and she touched the hollow at the base of her neck with still trembling fingers. Though still on crutches, every inch of him was just as deliciously handsome and powerfully strong as she remembered. He hobbled closer to her on his crutches.

"Why?" she asked, hope blooming in her heart, taking root in the recesses of her soul. A thousand bubbles seemed to flow through her veins and make her head spin, dizzying her in all the right ways.

"You left without saying goodbye and I needed to see you again," he said, stopping when they both reached each other.

Standing toe-to-crutched toe, he lifted one hand and caressed her face. "I want you to know that even if we can't have children of our own, I know we can still be a family."

Her throat closed, and her nose itched. Hot tears pricked behind her eyes. "How? I mean I guess adoption is an option, but that's a long process and there are no guarantees." A cool breeze caught a few loose strands of her hair, feathering them onto her cheeks. "I could hear it in your voice when you talked about how much you love your nieces and nephews. Family matters to you."

He warmed her face with his free palm, slid a bare thumb pad over her lips, stroking gently. "Family doesn't mean having a special set number of people in it to be real. Family can be two people being in love, growing old together, maybe touching other people's lives by being fabulous aunts, uncles, friends," he said softly, half-hopping closer to bridge the scant distance between them. "Maybe, one day, when I'm too old to carry a gun and I get sidelined, we can look into other ways to bring kids into our lives. But, you're the only family I need. You're the air I breathe, the sun shining in the darkest corners of my soul. You're light and joy and bring happiness to me. You're my family."

A tear escaped, and he brushed it away. "Brent, I left before saying goodbye and I also left before telling you the truth."

"You told me everything and I'm still here, aren't I?"

She flicked her glance away and caught site of another deer hovering in the woods beyond. Even further back, a stag stood tall. Protecting. Shielding his mate. Gathering her courage once more, she locked her eyes onto Brent's, determined to make things right. "I told you about the infertility, but I didn't come clean about my choices since the day of the accident."

"You had a lot to overcome," he said, lowering his head to hers.

"I did, but I've been using my work, my plans and career, to bury myself and hide from the world. From love. I didn't think I needed it, couldn't risk it." The air between them misted, warmed her face. She wrapped her hands around his neck, held onto him. Drew more strength. "I pushed you away after you told me the truth about why we met because..." she paused, inhaled a breath, and his masculine scent of woods and crisp clean winter sunshine wafted into her senses, enveloping her. Oh, how she loved the familiar, solidness of this man. Her man if she fought for him. "Deep down, I was afraid. Afraid to believe in love again and afraid of all the expectations that come from being with another person. I lost more than my husband and my baby on that day. I lost a big part of myself. Being with you brought that part alive again. And I don't want to live a half-life anymore. I'm sorry. So sorry for pushing you away."

"I should have told you. There's no getting around that truth, but I promise you with everything I have in me that I'll never keep you in the dark again," he said, brushing his lips onto her forehead, her cheeks, her mouth. "I can't tell you everything about my life, my missions, but I can give you what you need the most. Me. If you'll still have me."

A rustle of movement sounded behind her in the forest and the sun rays sparkled on invisible ice crystals. Slowly, she became aware of a crowd circling around them. Along with *Cooking Thyme's* crew, she spotted Alexandra, Spencer Caldwell and his fiancée. Their faces beamed and the family she'd always relied on became clear.

These were her people. They'd grown up with her and her brother, they'd celebrated with her when she'd emerged from the depths of despair and had landed her show.

And with Brent she could open a whole new world of possibilities.

"Yes," she said, caressing his cheek. "I'll have you."

A soft clapping sounded, and the crutches fell to the ground as Brent drew her into his arms and covered her mouth with his, bringing her home and to where she belonged.

With him. Now and forever.

*SIX MONTHS later*

Reagan's mother handed her the simple bouquet of Gerber daisies and springs of green leaves. "I'm so happy for you," she said with tears misting her light blue eyes. "Though we never thought we'd see this day arrive again, we hoped."

She smiled, then kissed her mother's still unlined cheek. "Neither did I, to be honest." But Brent had found a way into her heart, her life and her world. And she couldn't imagine moving forward without him by her side.

"He's a good man," her father added as he walked to stand beside her. "You ready to make him yours permanently?"

"Totally."

She took her parents' arms and together they strolled out of her room at Saxon's winery and down the stairway until they reached the bottom floor. Just outside, the man she'd fallen in love with waited for her to join him beneath the vine covered arbor set up next to the vineyard. Already, her brother and their friends, Spencer and Alexandra, had seated the small gathering of friends and family members.

Her heart filled when she heard the sounds of laughter, a baby's soft cry amidst the harp music playing. Once she'd had a wedding with all the stops pulled out: formal and perfect for then. And the rings she'd said her vows to when they were slipped onto her finger had bound to another good man. A man who would hold a special place in her heart for the rest of her life.

Those rings had never been replaced, but no one could erase what they'd given her.

Love.

And now she made her way to the man who'd shown her she could have love again. Brent.

As she moved toward him, saw his whiskey-colored eyes light up when she approached the altar, a floating sensation bubbled through her, filling her with renewed hope and wonder. Today she'd say her vows and cherish every new memory, every new moment with Brent.

And, after they'd finally exchanged a new set of rings, Brent lowered his mouth to hers, bringing her home all over again.

. . .

THANK you for reading Tempted by Her Rescuer! I hope you loved Reagan and Brent's story as much as I do. If you'd like to read more about her brother Colton and Isabella, dive into my new series Covert Rescuers' Undercover Shield/C.R.U.SH. today!

HERE'S an excerpt from the first CRUSH book, Covert Seduction...

SPECIAL AGENT COLTON SUTLER hated three things: the tuxedo currently strangling him, snakes, and drug dealing scumbags. No snakes in the grand ballroom —unless he counted the human one who might be at this historic manor house tonight. To secure an invitation, he had to call in a favor from Alexandra, the owner and a friend from his hometown in Virginia. One he hadn't talked to in forever.

Only tonight he hadn't come to party. He'd come to stop a monster.

He'd just wrapped up an investigation for the Drug Enforcement Agency when the intel came in about a suspect moving into Magnolia Falls' jurisdiction. Someone who'd surfaced as a connection to a case haunting him for three years.

Mario Rossi.

Colton was here to spy on the bastard, and finally get somewhere in a coveted drug investigation that cost his agency already too much time and lives. Now he had a chance to expose Mario and his crime boss. He'd learned they planned to import heroin to the region and Mario's boss planned to handle the details personally.

Colton could finally discover the brains behind this worldwide operation. He'd shut down the drug cartel and even the score on a personal level. His last operation in Magnolia Falls' had resulted in losing one of his best friends. He still blamed himself for the loss. This time no one he loved would die because of a deadly betrayal.

"Colton." Alexandra crossed the room and moved toward him, then brushed his cheeks one by one, European style. "I finally see you after all these years."

He smiled. She'd always been elegant with an air of sophistication even back in high school. Tonight, she exuded class in her strapless golden formal gown and her honey blonde hair swept into an elegant chignon. "It's been too long," he said, holding her hazel eyes with his.

"True." She lifted a glass of red wine from a passing server's tray. "I was surprised when you called, especially wanting to visit my winery, let alone attend my family's annual charity event. So not your thing."

"You'd be astonished by how much I've changed since you attended university overseas," he said, focusing on their past friendship revealing nothing about the real reason that brought him here.

And that reason still hadn't shown up at the gala. Not anywhere obvious. Had his informant been mistaken? Frustrated, he glanced at the dance floor where several guests swirled around the gleaming parquet surface. Some catchy pop song he hadn't heard before played and then a flash of red had him riveted on the woman twirling away from her partner's arms. Her smiling face, gorgeous and flushed, filled with laughter as she spun back into the man's body.

A slow burn simmered beneath the surface of his skin, catching him off guard. As did the thrumming of his pulse in his ears along with the instant attraction. He took another hit of his rich red wine and wished he'd chosen a crisp, cold chardonnay instead.

Her dance partner whirled her away from him again and before she could rebound into his waiting arms, her gaze collided with his. He locked onto the sultry dark eyes for a mouthwatering instant. Her lips parted, curved into another seductive smile just before her partner swiveled her away.

He swallowed another large gulp of wine. "Who's that woman?"

"Isabella Cavelli."

The hairs on the back of his neck raised. Her name sounded familiar, but he couldn't place it. Yet.

"Tell me more," he said, nodding toward the gorgeous brunette.

She switched dance partners, moving with grace over the floor despite the man's girth. He kept her in his sights.

"How'd you meet her?"

"She's one of my partners in a Global Winery Consortium to promote our wines. And she's become a friend," Alexandra said. "She owns a centuries' old vineyard in Tuscany and comes from a prosperous background." She placed her empty wineglass on a passing server's elegant silver tray without missing a beat, her movement as well-timed as a karate expert.

He tilted his head and stared at the dance floor. Adrenaline beat a tempo behind his ribcage. Mario Rossi grew up in Tuscany. He operated his primary resort on the coast near Isabella's winery. With declining harvests, did she have another source of income? "Sounds like she's on top of her game," Colton said, continuing to track her movements on the dance floor, mesmerized. Damn. He had to get his shit together. Mario might show up at any moment. But was he connected to Isabella somehow? He didn't recall her name showing up in any of his research before.

"Your sister Reagan told me about your business venture," Alexandra said, cutting into his thoughts. "I'm curious. Are you going to operate this venture from your office in Washington, D.C. or are you making this break a permanent one?"

His pulse accelerated, sending a drumbeat of wariness behind his sternum. If he hadn't known her throughout his childhood, he could have sworn she had more than a casual curiosity by her probing hazel eyes and carefully modulated tone of voice. Almost as if she didn't buy his cover story.

He swirled the wine in his glass, stalling until he had his heart rate and his unwarranted suspicion under control. His friend only wanted details about his return Magnolia Falls, and his pretense of taking over a bankrupt river rafting business. Part of him wanted to make his venture a reality. After all, his memories of growing up here made him nostalgic for easier, simpler times. Times when rafting the rivers and hiking the Shenandoah mountains while hanging out with his friends had given him a strong sense of security and love.

Unfortunately, the security had been false. Even this beautiful region had skeletons and problems lurking in the shadows of the sun-dappled pink rhododendrons, lush green forests, and acres of vineyards.

Which was why he'd committed himself to the DEA.

"Well?" she asked. "Are you moving back?"

"Not sure," Colton said. "Depends on how things

play out." He continued scanning the room for Mario.

"Getting more tourist money into the region will be good for the local economy," Alexandra said.

The prickling intensified as he continued to survey the room. No sign of the bastard yet. But his stomach clenched and his intuition beat a warning against his breastbone. The Italian socialite's attendance at his friend's charity gala couldn't be coincidental. Not when they came from the same region and could easily have run in the same social circles.

Mario Rossi would show up. Possibly to meet Isabella. Could she be the leader of Mario's cartel?

"Exactly," he said. "Hiring locally will bring a lot more cash into our hometown and the county." The right kind of money, not the kind that brought more crime and death into the area. Maybe after he wrapped up this case, he'd opt out of the DEA to follow through on his cover with real money. After he stopped the flow of tainted heroin—the street term white snow sounding innocent when the consequences of using were anything but—into the region and saved countless innocent lives.

But he didn't know how to be anything else. He'd miss the rush, the adrenaline of stopping criminals in their tracks.

People gathered in lines beside the buffet tables, but Mario wasn't among them. He hoped like hell this wasn't some god damn dead end. Colton had been tracking the drug dealer's movements, and they'd brought him here according to all his sources. Mario's boss wanted to oversee every detail. Bringing this person into custody meant everything to Colton. He trusted his sources. They'd never let him down before. Plus, his gut instinct confirmed his intel.

"We'll get more tourists into the area," Alexandra said.

He gave his former high school friend a sidelong glance. She'd been overseas throughout her university days and they'd lost touch. When he'd learned she'd returned to Magnolia Falls to run her family's vineyard following her mother's death, he'd been glad to hear she'd returned to her roots.

Roots meant something. And he aimed to safeguard his from getting spoiled before he returned to Washington to take on his next assignment.

"Is that Spencer Caldwell?" he asked, pointing to where his old friend danced with a leggy redhead.

"Yes. Hired him a few years ago."

"You convinced our local genius returned to Magnolia Falls to work for you?" he said. "He rocked the New York Stock Exchange."

"Money isn't the only thing that motivated Spencer to sign on with Saxon Vineyards," she said, then drank again.

"Oh?"

"He missed his family," she said matter-of-factly. "I offered him a way home."

"Nice." He briefly wondered if he'd find his way back to Magnolia Falls on a permanent basis, then pushed the wayward desire down deep to make small talk with Alexandra about local business to maintain his cover. "Your ongoing investments into updating historic Magnolia Falls will bump up the tourism numbers," he said, continuing to gaze at the dance floor.

The music's tempo ramped up to a bump and grind of 80s hits. Once more Isabella's dance partner spun her away from him, then brought her back to hold her close. She kept pace, matching him step-for-step.

Her sexy red dress swish-swooshed around her long legs, the hemline risque enough to draw some serious male appreciation and yet demure enough to convey a hint of innocence.

His collar seemed to strangle him and his groin tightened. *Damn it again. Keep your head in the game and get your cock out of the equation.* He was here for work and not pleasure. He undid the top button of his dress shirt to loosen it and killed the attraction with the last crime scene photos he'd processed.

The song ended, Isabella and her dance partner exited the parquet floor, then they made their way toward one of the wet bars tucked into the ballroom's corners.

He followed her movements, the sway of her full hips sending another rush of heat to his groin.

Alexandra nudged him. "Instead of drooling over her from a distance, you could just ask her to dance."

"Who?"

"Isabella. You've been watching her all night," Alexandra said while stopping another server to lift a new glass of wine from his tray. "Can't blame you. She's a trustworthy friend on top of being absolutely gorgeous."

"Yes. She's a real beauty."

"What's up with the sarcasm I hear in your voice?" Alexandra asked, then raised her glass and drank."

"Not sarcasm. Just figure she's out of my league."

She laughed. "Colton, I don't remember you ever having a problem getting a date."

"Well, you turned me down fifteen years ago." He'd liked her, admired her for more than her looks. He'd never considered her as a potential girlfriend until he'd had a particularly nasty breakup. She'd comforted him after he'd had one beer too many—as a friend. And then he'd made a first-class fool of himself.

"You didn't know what you were doing. Plus, you were a good friend back then," she said. "Go ahead. Ask her to dance. She's a super person with a heart of gold."

"You're right." He could use the opportunity to discover what her connection to Mario Rossi was until Mario showed up. "Think I'll slide the DJ a tip and tell him to play another slow song."

"Ha. Still can't get those two left feet of yours to cooperate?"

"What I've got in mind doesn't require stellar dancing ability," he said. "Catch you later."

Going into deep cover meant blurring the lines to get close to his enemies. Isabella probably had no connection to Mario, but he'd double his surveillance and run a quick background check on her before giving Isabella the all clear. And that meant the next dance she danced would be with him.

ISABELLA WIGGLED her toes in her Jimmy Choo's, trying to regain the feeling in the tips. She'd give anything to kick the damn things off, go to her room, read, and chill before her meeting with Alexandra tomorrow. Instead, she flashed a smile at—Tony? Tom?—who'd been sweet, but she didn't want to encourage him. Time to put the brakes on his interest.

"Thanks for dancing with me," she said.

"You sure you don't want to spend the rest of the night with me?" he asked, holding her gaze with slightly bleary eyes. "We'd be good together."

*Great. Scratch sweet.* "Aw. Only good? Sorry, not interested. I expect great when I go to bed with a guy," she said with an edge in her voice.

Tom-Tony's gaze narrowed. "Are you fucking kidding me?"

"No." Isabella stepped back, scanning the room for a quick escape and spotted her import-export rep milling with their clients. "I never kid around when it comes to my expectations."

He made a move toward her, but she jammed her spiked heel on top of his foot. "What the fuck?" He jumped away and bounced on his one good leg.

"My point exactly," she said. "*Arrivederci bastardo.*"

She swept around him and made her way toward her rep without bothering to look back.

"Good move," a masculine, deep voice said from behind her.

She stopped, turned around, and locked eyes with the man approaching her. "Old boarding school trick," she said. "Still comes in handy when guys try to go too far."

The sexy man who had been watching her while she danced with that idiot closed the remaining distance between them. "Shouldn't have to put up with that crap from anyone," he said. "You want me to boot the jerk out?"

"No reason to draw any negative attention to the event. We've raised a lot of money and positive awareness for the International Miracle Network," she said. "I'd rather keep the media's focus on the charity than put its lens on an ugly incident. He's taken care of."

"For now."

"And for later," she said. "The contract he hoped to sign with our company won't happen. That'll be tough to explain to his superiors at Vincenzo Resorts. Might even cost him his job." Isabella held her head high and locked her gaze onto his. "What's your name?"

"Colton Sutler." He stretched his hand.

Ah, the accountant from D.C. Alexandra had mentioned in passing. Someone Alexandra had known in high school. Clearly, not someone she needed to worry about.

Isabella took his hand and shook it. A tingling sensation traveled along her skin, then arrowed deeper. Did this handsome guy always make hearts race? Most likely. "I'm Isabella," she said, pulling her hand from his and rubbing her arm to erase the sudden sparks.

Colton cocked his head to the side and lifted a brow. "You always this mercenary with overzealous dance partners?"

"Only when it's necessary."

The air crackled between them, overriding the clinking glasses and party chatter. He held her gaze. "I like a woman who knows how to handle her affairs, Isabella."

She inhaled his woodsy, dark scent and more awareness sizzled along her nerve-endings. Oh, he'd be more than great in bed. Probably beyond impressive. But she didn't casually hook up with guys no matter how appealing, especially not with a man who exuded a powerful ruggedness despite the tuxedo contouring his broad shoulders to perfection.

"Speaking of *business*." Not affairs or anything remotely sounding like getting between the sheets with someone. "I'd like to continue mingling with the guests to drum up more donations for the charity."

"Another excellent idea," he said, then smiled. "Mind if I join you? You know, just in case another jerk tries to come at you. I can be your pro bono bodyguard."

"Why would you be pro bono?"

"Because I'm still in training. Need experience."

His grin reached his pewter rimmed gray eyes, turning them into liquid silver. Her heart hopscotched inside her chest. Not good. Not good at all. Colton Sutler did things to her carefully guarded libido, but that didn't mean she wanted to brush him off. She pressed her palm against her sternum and waited for her pulse to slow down. Spending the evening with a guy like him wouldn't upend her carefully laid plans for the future.

Plans that kept her on the straight and narrow after coming close to losing everything she'd worked for during her senior year in university.

"Fine. I'll help you with that only because I'm feeling charitable tonight," she said, smiling and lighthearted despite still searching for a way to diffuse the attraction pinging between them. "But first I'd like to speak with my public relations person. We haven't touched base since the silent auction. She's over there." Isabella pointed to her pretty American colleague, Jillian Baxter, whom she'd hired over a year ago to expand her promotions and marketing into the US marketplace. Jillian's ebony curls with light highlights framed her tawny brown face as she stood by the buffet at the opposite side of the expansive ballroom. Her spirals danced as Jillian nodded, laughed while chatting animatedly with a man whose back blocked the rest of Isabella's view.

"Looks like she's occupied with someone else."

"Probably a potential donor or contact," she said. "I should go."

"How about I walk you there, then grab some food while I wait for you to wrap up," he said easily. "You know., so I'll be close by as your pro bono body-guard in case you run into trouble."

A laugh bubbled inside her. This guy seemed legitimately fun. And she hadn't had a whole lot of fun lately. "Sure. If I need your assistance, I'll snap my fingers."

"Awesome. Let's go over then."

They walked side-by-side with mere millimeters separating them as they made their way to the banquet tables. Though they didn't touch each other, electricity crackled and sparked over her bare skin.

Then the charges zipped beneath the surface into her nipples, making them pebble into tight points.

Her nerves jangled, but no way would she let Colton see how much he'd affected her.

Then the man talking with Jillian turned around and the familiar face sent a wave of relief through her. "Mario," she said, quickening her pace.

Colton kept up with her. "You know that guy?"

"Oh, we've been friends since we were kids. Like *famiglia*," she hastened to add before they reached Mario.

"I didn't know you'd be here." She embraced Mario and kissed his cheeks one-by-one. "Alexandra didn't tell me."

Mario's expensive cologne wafted into her nostrils, another familiar touch point and she inhaled it gratefully. "Actually, I told her to hold off. I wanted to surprise you, darling." Mario held her at arms' length and laughter crinkled the corners of his espresso colored eyes.

"*I* wanted to tell you ages ago, but Mario insisted we wait until he could tell you in person."

Isabella looked at one, then the other. "Wait. Are you two?"

"Dating?" Jillian shot Mario a sultry look with slanted amber eyes. "Yes. We met at a food and wine conference a few months ago."

"Well, this is a crazy coincidence," Isabella said. "But a nice one." She genuinely wanted her friends to be happy. Though the fact that they were an item caught her off guard.

"Definitely." Mario tugged Jillian a little closer and kissed her temple. "I had no idea she worked for you until after we… connected."

"And well, we never knew how long this would last, but here we are," Jillian said, twining her fingers through Mario's hair. "I hope this isn't a problem for you."

"No," Isabella said, moving a little closer to Colton despite her desire to keep men at a distance until she'd established her career. "Not at all." Truthfully, seeing her colleague's happiness made her wistful for her own.

Another ballad piped through the speakers, Jillian looked up at Mario. "I love *Slow Hands*," she said.

"I know," Mario said, stroking her arm until he linked hands with her. "Let's dance, *tesoro*."

"Join us," she said over her shoulder as they moved toward the parquet floor. "It'll be fun."

"Sounds good," Colton said before Isabella could protest, turning to glance her way. "I'm game. Are you?" He shot her a charm-the panties-off-a-girl grin.

*Yes. Yes. Yes.* Her hormones hummed to life, making her head spin. "Absolutely," she said after a beat of hesitation. After all, she could handle her urges during one song. "But then I'm done. My feet are killing me."

Isabella took his hand. Her skin sizzled at the contact, igniting sparks. They licked their way into every erogenous zone she possessed. By the time he wrapped his arms around her and drew her into his muscular body, the flames discovered places she'd forgotten existed.

COLTON SWAYED WITH ISABELLA, close, but not too close or he'd let his other brain do all the talking. Around them, other couples crowded the floor and he could see Jillian cozying up with Mario, leaving no doubt about what she had planned for the rest of the night.

"Your PR rep is nice," he said, wondering about the connection between Mario and Isabella besides being childhood friends.

"Yes. She's excellent at her job. I'm glad I hired her."

He held her slender waist, resisted the urge to cruise his palms down her full hips and over her incredible ass. "That's crazy how she hooked up with your friend at a conference," he said with a fake note of incredulity in his voice.

"Hmmmm. Small world."

"Yes." The coincidence didn't escape Colton's radar. After everything he'd been through in the field, he questioned anything happening by chance. What was Isabella's real connection to Mario? Most people who knew him were on the wrong side of the law in a bad way. Only a fool would believe she didn't know the real Mario.

But maybe not. She seemed genuinely amazed when she spotted Mario in the crowd. Still, she could be part of the drug cartel—his partner. Perhaps even the person directing the entire operation. "How long have you two known each other?" he asked, though he'd crosscheck anything she told him with a database search afterward.

"Oh years. Our parents...," her voice trailed off and her shoulders stiffened, then she shrugged. "Let's just say we have a lot in common and leave it at that."

Interesting. Mario's family had been embroiled in an international embezzlement scandal when he'd been a kid. As had another fashion icon and her husband. Colton searched his memory and bam... He connected the dots. Isabella's parents had also been arrested and jailed for a time. "Yeah. Like you're both Italian, and he's in the hospitality business," he said, not betraying his thoughts. "You supply his hotels and resorts with your wines too?"

She twined her arms around his neck and turned her head to glance over at her friends. "We have a contract with Rossi Resorts and Spas," she said quietly. "Our way—my brother and me—of maintaining our families' prior business connections while showing the world that the Cavelli/Rossi names are synonymous with honest transactions."

Not Mario Rossi's. Not given the last bit of intel he'd received before returning to Magnolia Falls. "Now?" he asked. "You mean they weren't before?"

She stiffened ever so slightly. "No. But I don't like to think about those days."

He could imagine why. Isabella would have been almost ten-years-old when the scandal made the news. She'd disappeared off the paparazzi's radar shortly before they had announced the prison sentences. "I understand." He brought her closer to him. A huge part of him hated bringing up her history... her voice had gone flat, lost its sparkle when she'd replied. "Glad things have changed for the better."

"After my grandfather saved our vineyards and restore our finances, my brother and I busted our tails to maintain our family's reputation." She swished her head back to meet his gaze. "Trust is our watchword."

He inhaled more of her delicious aroma. Damn. She smelled good—like an exotic perfume but not too bold.

Light. Expensive. Elegant.

But despite his inclination to go with his gut and believe her, he couldn't relax his standards. Not after what had happened three years ago when he'd been betrayed by the woman he'd been with while undercover. Danger could lurk beneath the understated perfume.

"Song's ending," she said as the last notes played through the speakers. "Thanks for the dance."

He caught Jillian and Mario leaving the dance floor and tracked their exit all the way to a hallway leading to the manor house's grand foyer. Knowing Mario had been given a suite of rooms while staying at the winery's manor house, Colton decided to stick with Isabella. Because he had to make sure her story checked out. "How about we go for another round?" he asked.

She broke their contact and pointed to her shoes. "My feet need a break, remember? Plus, you've just reminded me I need to talk with Mario before he leaves the party."

An alarm rang in his ears, flashed a neon warning in his mind's sight. The daughter of criminals meeting with the son of criminals? Another non-coincidence. No way would he let her out of his sight. "You always all business?" he asked as he escorted her off the floor.

"Not at all. I want to thank him for making sure my parents are well-taken care of while my brother and I are in the States." She stopped walking and leaned against a white pillar. "They're staying at his resort in Tuscany. My father's health isn't good ever since his heart attack last year. Mario offered to have his staff look after them, discreetly. My parents are proud people, especially Papa."

"Nice of him," Colton said. But he doubted the bastard had a decent bone in his body.

"Mario's a great guy. He helped me out of a few jams when I attended college. We look after each other." She grabbed a glass of wine from a server's tray and sipped. "Thanks again for wanting to get rid of that jerk for me. And for the dance."

The adrenaline rushing through his veins charged into his extremities. Jams meant trouble. And he knew the kind of trouble Mario circumvented. Colton lowered his head to study her more closely, trying to read her dark brown eyes for anything else in them. "Maybe I'll see you around the vineyard next week," he said after discovering nothing suspicious other than a hint of pain glimmering in their depths.

"Perhaps," she said. "*Ciao*, Colton." Isabella kissed both his cheeks, then scooted around him.

Shit. She'd just given him a polite, cool friendly brush off. He turned on his heel to go trail her. His eyes locked on her sensually swaying hips and the bright red dress that flirted against her long legs. She'd be easy to find in that dress.

He'd come here to tail a monster and discover the drug lynch pin's ringleader. Now he had a big wrinkle to smooth out. Things had gotten a lot more complicated. The woman he was attracted to could be the leader of the most dangerous drug cartels in the world.

And he'd stop at nothing to stop the cartel from gaining a foothold in this region.

KEEP READING COVERT SEDUCTION TODAY...

The Tycoon's Red Hot Marriage Merger

The Marriage Ultimatum

**The Red Hot Hero Series**

Red Hot Fling: Red Hot Heroes 1

Red Hot Reunion: Red Hot Heroes 2

Red Hot Proposal: Red Hot Heroes 3

**Be the first to hear about my new releases.**

There's all kinds of fun ways to get connected and exclusive giveaways too!

**Christine's Newsletter**

## ABOUT CHRISTINE

*USA Today* Bestselling Author Christine Glover writes sexy, intriguing contemporary romances. She loves discovering how her determined heroines and super sexy heroes with heart journey toward their own happily ever afters. Her characters are real people from all walks of life who embody classic love stories with a modern twist. She enjoys finding the silly in the serious, making wine out of sour grapes, and giving people giggle fits along with heartfelt hugs. When she's not writing, you can find her traveling the world, cooking gourmet food, and desperately seeking a corkscrew.

If you enjoyed this book and would like to leave an honest review, Christine would really appreciate it because that's how other readers discover their new Happily Ever Afters.

*Hang Out with Christine*

Sign Up for Christine's Newsletter
Join Christine's Street Team

www.christineglover.com
christinegloverauthor@gmail.com

- facebook.com/ChristineGloverAuthor
- twitter.com/cjglover63
- bookbub.com/authors/christine-glover
- pinterest.com/cjglover63

# ACKNOWLEDGMENTS

Many thanks to my incredible critique partners, Pam Mantovani and Carmen Falcone. You make me a better writer with your honesty and support!

Big shout out to my readers and the CRUSHES! You're the reason I sit in my chair for hours, alone in a room to write these love stories. Plus, I love chatting with all of you every chance I can get!

Major appreciation goes to my fabulous family and friends. They keep me sane, bring me chocolate and wine, and joy!! Lots of joy. My world is better because you're in it with me.

BROTHERHOOD PROTECTORS

ORIGINAL SERIES BY ELLE JAMES

## ABOUT ELLE JAMES

ELLE JAMES also writing as MYLA JACKSON is a *New York Times* and *USA Today* Bestselling author of books including cowboys, intrigues and paranormal adventures that keep her readers on the edges of their seats. With over eighty works in a variety of sub-genres and lengths she has published with Harlequin, Samhain, Ellora's Cave, Kensington, Cleis Press, and Avon. When she's not at her computer, she's traveling, snow skiing, boating, or riding her ATV, dreaming up new stories. Learn more about Elle James at www.ellejames.com

Website | Facebook | Twitter | GoodReads | Newsletter | BookBub | Amazon

*Follow Elle!*
www.ellejames.com
ellejames@ellejames.com

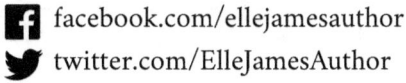

facebook.com/ellejamesauthor
twitter.com/ElleJamesAuthor